AGATHA

AGATHA

William L. Truax III

Copyright © 2019 by William L. Truax Iii. All rights reserved.

No part of this publication may be reproduced, stored in a retrieval system or transmitted in any way by any means, electronic, mechanical, photocopy, recording or otherwise without the prior permission of the author except as provided by USA copyright law.

This novel is a work of fiction. Names, descriptions, entities, and incidents included in the story are products of the author's imagination. Any resemblance to actual persons, events, and entities is entirely coincidental.

The opinions expressed by the author are not necessarily those of URLink Print and Media.

1603 Capitol Ave., Suite 310 Cheyenne, Wyoming USA 82001
1-888-980-6523 | admin@urlinkpublishing.com

URLink Print and Media is committed to excellence in the publishing industry.

Book design copyright © 2019 by URLink Print and Media. All rights reserved.

Published in the United States of America

ISBN 978-1-64367-414-8 (Paperback)
ISBN 978-1-64367-413-1 (Digital)

03.05.19

TO TIFFANY WHO HELPED ME ALONG THE WAY.

CHAPTER 1

The house was white, newer model, it had a blue trim and two windows on either side of it with a door in the dead center. The house was relatively small but looked rather homely. You could tell it was either recently built or recently painted because it glistened in the moonlight. There was a candle in the far-right side window. From the street it looked fake (due to its bright yellow color and ghostly appearance), but as you got closer to the window you noticed that the flame was real, and that the candlestick was just that bright of a white.

Agatha lived in this house. She enjoyed every moment that she could possibly spend here. She enjoyed the moments of watching television, reading books and web browsing. Everything you could ever imagine doing inside of a home she did so in hers, and she did one thing extra that other people don't normally do in theirs... She channeled the LIVING.

The latest LIVING beings that Agatha channeled was for a dear friend Benita who happened to be her next-door neighbor. Her husband, daughter and son each took turns telling Benita that they'll see her soon and that she should keep herself happy and warm. The look on her face said it all, and Benita (once her family was gone) paid Agatha her small fee for the happiness that Agatha brought.

One-night Agatha stood in the kitchen of her little white house and peered over the counter-tops trying to catch a glimpse of the television while preparing dinner for herself. While she was cutting carrots, one of her fingers got in the way and she accidentally cut right through it! Before freaking out she picked up her hand and stared at it, and just blew on it and POOF! The tip of her finger was back on it. No harm, no foul.

While Agatha was eating dinner, a sudden ring on her cell phone made her jump. This ringtone was designated to a person, a florist that she had a huge crush on. This person would call once or twice a month just to check in on her, get the latest gossip or tell her to come by the shop so that she can get a bouquet of flowers. With each ring, Agatha's heart leapt into her throat.

"I Want You Back" by 'N Sync kept playing on a loop. Finally drumming up the nerve she pressed the answer button and was greeted with a loud batch of white noise.

"Hello?" Agatha heard no response. She shrugged it off, thinking that signals had crossed somewhere on the line. She hung up the phone and went back to her meal. Almost immediately the phone rang a second time. Same contact, same ringtone. Agatha was once again greeted with white noise.

"H... hello?" she said hesitantly. This time Agatha listened closer and heard a faint voice through the noise. She jerked the phone away from her ear, threw it on the table and shoved herself as far from the table as she possibly could. After taking a moment to calm down, she shakily picked up her phone and ended the call.

Agatha slowly stood and made her way down the hall. The walls were lined with pictures of relatives and close friends. There were so many that the eggshell colored walls were barely visible. She had considered removing those of people estranged from her, but she didn't have the heart. Those were her memories.

She made her way into her study which had a computer, a rocking chair and a bookcase full of books. The bookcase was only five shelves high but still it was full.

The rocking chair was antique, wooden and very comfortable to sit in. The computer in the room was on a white four-foot-long table. It was plastic, not too cheap and not too expensive. It was one of those jobbers you found at hardware stores. She had a chair that was black leather, had four wheels on it and was very comfy to sit on, it rocked and had a squeak to it every so often.

She pulled a chair out from under the table and sat in front of her laptop, opened it up and turned it on. It took about 10 seconds before it booted to the Windows loading screen, another 15 seconds until she could enter in her password, and then 30 more seconds for it to finally load into Windows itself on her desktop. Agatha had this habit of timing her computer. She was always trying to keep it under one minute of load time, 55 seconds isn't too bad she thought.

She heard that song playing once more, so she rushed out to the kitchen grabbed the phone off the table there and answered it. Again, she was greeted by white noise.

"What's going on?" Agatha said out loud her voice strained a bit.

A little bewildered but not overly concerned just yet, she grabbed her phone and went back into the study. She looked at the walls in the study and noticed that they were brown with little black streaks going up and down and she thought that she needed to paint them, not tonight but soon.

Agatha sat in front of the computer and opened her favorite web browser Internet explorer, and began searching for 'white noise, cell phone, live call'.

Her search pulled back 28 million results in .28 seconds. She couldn't believe how many people had the same problem. That's when she started to really look at it and noticed that none of it had to do with the cell phone, most of it had to do with white noise on TV or white noise on the regular landline phone. Nothing about cell phones, she was rather disturbed about that.

So, she went to her cell phone company's website, signed in and went to the forums and made a post about her extraordinary event that happened three times tonight.

When she was done typing she returned her attention to a very friendly website Facebook. She was there to play catch-up with some old friends and play the games. She also went there to see if anyone knew about this white noise thing that was going on with her cell phone. Sadly no one was online, and she could not ask anyone directly. So, she made a post about four lines long:

> "Dear friends and anyone who reads this,
> I have been experiencing some intermittent issues with my cell phone, it sounds like white noise, static, anyone know anything about that? If you know anything let me know,"

She clicked post and knew it was going to take a little while before she got any results. Agatha was a patient person, so she could wait it out. Then she went back to her normal browsing and playing video games on Facebook and when Agatha was done and tired, she went to bed leaving her computer up and running not thinking anything of it.

He cupped her face in his hands as she leaned over the table and closed her eyes. Her hands fell to his face and then they moved down to his shoulders. She traced his arms all the way to his hands.

"I love you, you know. There could be no one else other than you Dorian and I can't imagine anyone in my life but you," Agatha said as sexy as she could to him.

Dorian smiled and leaned in and pressed his lips against hers as hard and passionately as he could. Agatha melted in his grasp, she felt that if she could fly from her mortal body that she would soar as high as the eagles and she would never have to land. Besides, Dorian would be right there next to her to catch her if she fell.

Dorian rose from the table clasping her hand in his. He tugged on it gently and she stood up, they pushed their chairs in and made their way out of the little white house. Agatha closed the door, locked it up behind her and took a glance back at it to make sure everything was safe. She then walked down to the sidewalk and got into Dorian's Nissan Altima.

As Dorian rounded the car and slid into the driver's seat, he reminded her to buckle up while he was doing it himself.

Agatha smelled the inside of the car and thought that it smelled funny, kind of like rotting flesh and death. When she brought it to Dorian's attention he claimed it was from the fish that he had in the car the day before.

"What are you worried about?"

"I guess nothing, I didn't mean to offend you Dorian. I am so sorry," Agatha said with a sad puffy face. Her eyes slightly watered and she felt a little embarrassed.

Dorian turned the key to his Altima and the beast roared to life. He pressed the gas a couple of times revving the engine up while looking over at Agatha and smiling at her. Agatha rolled her eyes and just looked away.

"You know that's really not all that impressive," she said to him with a matter-of-fact tone.

Dorian's smile faded quickly and looked rather annoyed. He shifted the gear into drive and sped off leaving behind him a cloud of dust with Agatha sitting beside him screaming her head off yelling for him to stop.

He got to the end of the street after passing numerous parked cars and vacant houses and lived-in-homes all various sizes shapes and colors, but at that stop sign he looked at her and asked her a very simple question....

"You're mine, right?"

"What do you mean by that Dorian? As of right now we are still a couple if that's what you mean, but with the way you're acting I'm not sure for how much longer that's going to be,"

He leaned in and kissed Agatha on her cheek and apologized for his behavior. He told her that he would be closer to himself than what he had been for the rest of the night. He told her things would work out better here in a little bit.

Dorian then turned left at the stop sign towards the woods and towards an unknown destination.

The lights on the road flickered as they drove towards the woods. It bothered Agatha a bit, but at the same time it didn't bother her at all. She kept her eyes front and sometimes out the passenger side window looking for deer or other animals that would cross the path of the car. She spied an armadillo, a couple possums, and a group of raccoon's rummaging through some of the trash cans that were down at the side of the road.

The headlights spied an old man wearing an orange polo shirt and a pair of blue jeans walking up the road. Agatha started tapping Dorian's arm saying that they should stop and pick up the old man and bring him to wherever he's going. But Dorian just drove right past him completely ignoring the old man.

A quarter mile up the road from where they passed the old man was a turn that Dorian took a little too sharply and nearly flipped the car. While it was up on what felt like its two wheels, Dorian began to panic and hollered for Agatha to hold on, and she in return began freaking out all over him.

Once the car settled Dorian came to an abrupt stop.

He placed one arm over her seat and before he could say anything she slapped the daylights out of him.

"What in the world were you thinking Dorian? You could've killed us both!" she shouted at him.

He hung his head down and had a slight smirk show across it, "It's not my fault that I want to show off for you," he replied with a more devious smile.

Agatha just stared at him, not sure what to make of this "NEW" Dorian. These new looks, new traits, new everything. Everything about him had changed. His dark mahogany hair was a stark contrast to the blonde it had been when they met. His physique had also changed. He once had an average build and slight belly, but now he has built up long and lean muscle. This wasn't necessarily odd to Agatha, except for the fact that the timing was unnatural. He had built as much muscle in days that would take other people weeks or even months. He was always open and willing to listen, but in the last few weeks he had become more closed off, calculated and cold. In fact, the only thing about Dorian that had not changed were his eyes. They were still the mesmerizing deep, emerald green eyes that she could fall into. Yet, there was a new glint behind those eyes that troubled Agatha.

"What's the matter Aggie, don't trust me or something?"

"It's not that Dorian," she stared at him nearing the terrified point and ready to jump from the vehicle, "please take me home, I'd like to go home,"

"Sorry, no can do. You're mine now and you're not going anywhere," he stated and locked the car doors and just smiled at her. That smile sent shivers down Agatha's spine.

'What have I gotten myself into now, what am I going to do, how am I going to get out of this?' her thoughts were focused but chaotic at the same time.

Dorian started driving once again and the thoughts of her death were becoming more realistic, but still, she pushed them aside thinking that Dorian would snap out of this spell he was under and save her and himself.

The tree line edged ever nearer, soon it seemed as if it were on top of them. 'At least it gives a warning,' she thought. Agatha looked around the car for something that she could use to save herself with, but like usual Dorian kept a clean car. There was nothing on the floorboard, not even a wrapping paper from a piece of candy. She glanced to the back seat thinking that if people don't keep their garbage up front, it may be in the back behind the seats…nothing, clean as a whistle.

Agatha felt a surprising weight fall on top of her as they passed the tree line. She looked over at Dorian who seemed to be more focused on getting her to their destination than before. Terror buried itself inside her mind and body, but she retained control. She wanted to remember every aspect of the scene.

Dorian reached over to stroke her hair and she recoiled from him and slapped at his hand.

The mountains overcast their shadows on top of the vehicle and the surrounding area making it feel cooler and appear darker than what it was already. Dorian put the high beams on and the Nissan Altima began to take the beginning steps of a long bend in the road. Agatha stared out the windshield and thought about various ways to escape but nothing stuck and then she spied an old man in an orange polo shirt walking once more on the road.

"Dorian, haven't we seen this man before?" she asked. No response.

"DORIAN! Are you LISTENING?!"

"Yes, I was looking. No, I don't see anyone but the road." He said as calmly as he could.

Agatha looked back out the windshield and the old man was gone, so she looked out her side window and she was greeted with white eyes and a white jagged smile. She watched as these eyes and teeth moved like they were speaking to her and just as fast as they formed, they vanished from sight.

Her screams burrowed deep inside Dorian's ears and it caused him to jerk the car and pull it over.

"What's wrong?" he screamed at her.

"The old man…gone…his eyes…his smile! Something's not… right… with him," Agatha said between gasps of air.

Dorian looked back and there was no one nor anything behind them.

Dorian scratched his head and said to Agatha that he was going to grab a light from the glove compartment and look around. He reached over her, and she latched onto his arm and refused to release it.

"No, you can't go, it'll kill you!" she screamed.

"I must, I have to see what has you so scared and defeat it," 'Now you're my hero.' Agatha thought.

Dorian stepped out of the car and left it running so that Agatha had the air conditioning for a little comfort. He clicked on the small black metallic flashlight and began shining it in various directions, focusing on the road the most. To his left he heard some rustling in the brush, so he pointed his trusty flashlight in that direction and out hopped a rabbit.

He stayed out there for a little while looking all over and did not find anything. So, he went back inside the vehicle and put it back into gear and continued his way to this unknown place…

Agatha was tenser than ever. She began asking questions and Dorian was having none of it.

"Why can't you be quiet for a few and relax? I'm not a stranger, am I?"

"I guess not Dorian,"

"So, relax some,"

They arrived at the park and a foreboding feeling comes over Agatha, but she shakes it off and tries to focus on bringing back Dorian to himself.

"We're here Aggie, come, the park will close soon," he said getting out of the car. He walked over to her side and opened the door. Agatha got out and Dorian took her by the hand guiding her to the swings.

Dorian pushed Agatha on the swings for a while and sang to her. He had a lovely singing voice. After a while, he realized that Agatha seemed to be in a better mood which is what he wanted.

She giggled and squealed with every push. She jumped off the swing and landed on her feet with a very shaky landing.

"I haven't done that since I was a kid," she commented. "Neither have I, should I give it a go?"

"Not unless you want a little pain in your legs and feet,"

Dorian shrugged his shoulders and walked up to her pulling her in close to kiss her cheek. She smiled and laid her head down on his shoulder and kissed his exposed neck.

"Dorian,"

"Yes,"

"What are your plans with me tonight?"

"I'm taking you somewhere special to me and the rest is a surprise. I know you'll love it! Come, let's get moving," Dorian grabbed Agatha's hand and began the long walk up the hill.

Darkness quickly enclosed them, there was no escaping it. Dorian pulled out the flashlight he had before and guided the two of them up the hill to where the destination lay waiting.

The trees were thick, and the grass was majorly overgrown in desperate need of mowing. There were sounds of multiple types of crickets and frogs and many other creatures. A bat swooped down collecting a few insects and nearly landed in Agatha's hair. Agatha screamed periodically with each new sound and trembled with others. Dorian thought it was cute that she was not an outdoor girl.

Suddenly, as if the doors of time opened, the trees parted and there was a long, shimmering, polished white granite stone before them. There was a red cloth in the center of it and on either end, there were what looked to be straps.

"I'm not into bondage,"

"I know," he smiled, "it's not for you,"

She looked puzzled. He grabbed her wrist and suddenly a white rag came out of his pocket and covered her mouth.

Her eyes felt heavy and she felt woozy, tired, beyond exhausted. She found herself falling into Dorian's arms and the next thing that she recalls is waking for a moment while being tied to the rock.

"Why…are…you…do…ing…this?"

"Why? Soon you will know, for now sleep," he said.

Agatha laid on the stone barely breathing, her short rapid breaths slightly concerned Dorian. He leaned over her and placed his head on her chest and listened intently to her heartbeat.

"Perfectly fine, she'll wake soon, and they'll arrive by then. All is going according to plan,"

Soon after, two men in green and black arrived and pulled out a dagger each, placing it on the Altar at Agatha's abdomen. They then saluted and bowed to Dorian in an old gentlemanly fashion. Dorian returned the bow and smiled.

Twelve times he did this, and twelve different daggers appeared before Agatha's body.

She began to stir. Agatha heard sounds of voices talking in joyful conversations. She wondered where she was and what she was doing, but she couldn't open her eyes and her hearing was just starting to come in.

"She's waking, your eminence,"

"Finally! The festival can officially begin, our guest of honor is here!" Dorian proclaimed raising his arms.

Just as he began to turn to look at Agatha, a man in a diamond studded jacket called out to him.

"Lord, why must we eat of this fruit?"

"It is our right and she is our savior. We must all take part, you know what you are doing and when to do it. Be brave," Dorian placed a hand on the man's shoulders and patted it gently, "tonight's our night. The WORLD will be ours!"

They both smiled at each other and Dorian began to move towards Agatha, popping his fingers as he walked. He had a smile on his face that the devil himself would find offensive.

He arrived at the stone and looked at her with a deadly grin.

"Your time is coming my dear. Be strong and you may survive this... then again, you may not," He picked up a dagger and a crowd of people instantly flocked to him...

With a heavy hand, Dorian raised the dagger high into the air, and like lightning, the dagger struck deep into her left shoulder. Agatha let out a scream and it echoed throughout the surrounding woods. Blood squirted and drizzled, pouring down the knife blade.

He picked up another dagger and went down to her feet. Once more he raised a different dagger high into the air and again it came crashing down but this time into her foot and another one into the other foot. He made his way up to the right shoulder and there too he stabbed a dagger into her.

The crowd of people cheered and were applauding his actions and chanting something that Agatha could not make out. The sheer amount of pain she was in was all that she could comprehend in that moment.

Suddenly she felt a deep, slow, arching pain that entered through her abdomen and pierced down towards her spine. The pain was even more severe than the pain from being stabbed in the shoulders and feet. Her mouth opened wide and she gasped for air and tried to let out a scream, but it was muffled by a white cloth of some sort.

The man holding the white cloth began chuckling and she then began biting down on the cloth trying to rip it apart, but it seemed to be useless.

Dorian raised his hand once more on the opposite side of her body and sliced into her once again. Leaving the six daggers in her body, Dorian picked up the remaining six daggers and placed them alongside her. Six men from the crowd stepped forward and each of them picked up a dagger and with a synchronized motion they delivered the final blow.

Agatha woke with a series of pains in her body. She felt every knife wound all over again. Her phone began ringing and once more white noise. This no longer surprised her, but it was still confusing.

She made her way into the bathroom and stood behind the door facing the long, six-foot mirror. She barely fit inside of it, but she could see all of herself. From her auburn hair (that was in desperate need of a brushing) to her hazel eyes (that leaned more to being gray than hazel). To her athletic build which she was very proud of.

She raised her shirt and noticed that the wounds from the knives were bleeding yet again. From the knife wound in the center of her head, to the wounds on her size 34B breasts, down to her thighs and one on her inner thigh. She couldn't quite explain it, but this happened quite often.

She began bandaging herself, wrapping with a white ace bandage wrap over her wounds when her phone began to ring. 'I'll let it go to voicemail, see there's white noise then,' she thought to herself. Eventually the phone silenced itself and there was a beeping sound about a minute later which notified Agatha of a voicemail.

While Agatha was bandaging her wounds, she wondered why she kept dreaming of that night. It was not a night that she wanted to relive. She thought about Dorian and realized how much she missed him. Even though Dorian's betrayal caused her death, somewhere in her heart she still loved him.

There was a loud knocking sound at the front door. The knocking sound rounded every corner all the way into the bathroom. It was loud like a policeman's knock, but that wasn't quite right, it did not have the same style to it. It was short three bursts and then three hard thumps, and then there was silent for about a moment or two and then it repeated.

Agatha was not completely bandaged up when she rushed out to the door. She peered out the peephole and looked at the man that stood there. He was rather distorted but that was to be expected, he seemed tall, dressed in blue, and he had on a blue hat as well.

"Hello sir, what can I do for you?"

"Are you Agatha? I am here on the behest of Dorian, he is here with us and demands your presence."

"Well you can tell Dorian that I am done with him," she said a little peeved.

"Agatha, your life has not had purpose until this moment, now that we have found you, once more your life has purpose—a meaning. Come with me and we can show you your purpose," the man in blue said trying to be convincing.

Agatha was getting very upset with this man at her door. She looked down and noticed that she had her phone in her hand and said through the door that she was going to call the police if he did not get off her porch and leave her alone. The man said that he would leave, and he did, while he was walking away he said that others would be back to pick her up, that this was not the end.

Agatha stepped away from the door after a few minutes, making sure that the man was good and gone. She sat down on her brown sofa and turned her phone on to listen to the message. She held down the one-button and typed in her password for the voicemail service and listened to Dorian's message:

"Aggie, I have found myself in need of a partner, I need you and all of your 'channeling' expertise. I do hope that you can forgive me and others who took part in your untimely demise, but it was all part of a greater plan.

Do call me back, I do need you very much, and I will always love you,"

Agatha didn't delete the message, she just scoffed at it and hung up the phone. She got off the couch and went back into the bathroom where she finished placing the bandages on her body. Once she was done, she headed into the kitchen and made breakfast. Trying to get her day off to a better start than what it had been so far, she made herself bacon and eggs with the bacon smiling at her on the plate.

While she was eating she popped on Constantine and thought to herself that she could play the role of Constantine a lot better than the actor that portrays him does. After all she does channel the LIVING for a living.

Her house phone rang (which was her business phone) wildly until she picked it up.

"LIVING CHANNELS! Aggie speaking, how may I help you?"

Agatha listened intently to the other end of the phone, but it was silent, she pressed the receiver against her ear tighter, but still no sound. 'Why would my phone ring and then go silent mysteriously?' She thought in frustration.

Suddenly someone came walking through her front door and propped themselves at her kitchen table, turned and faced her and just stared. Agatha saw his eyes and his eyes were terrifying. They were crimson color with a hint of white in the center that glowed fiercely. He was in a gray and white pair of pants and shirt, like a jogger's uniform, and he wore a red visor.

He tried to speak but it was all garbled up, Agatha was very unsure of what to do. For the most part, she stared at the man while she tried to figure out what he was trying to say.

Just as suddenly as the man bursting in, Benita her next-door neighbor and friend, decided to drop by and pay a visit as well. Without knocking, she too walked right through the door sat down at the kitchen table and just stared at Agatha with the same eyes as the man sitting across from her.

Agatha was instantly terrified. She had been scared before, but now all her senses were dramatically heightened. She was on high alert. She felt like Spider-man, just without the webbing and superpowers.

They were both rambling the same incoherent sentences, it sounded something like this:

Church, stabbing, New God, Christ Child, worship, pigs, cats, Rape of Eve.

There were other things, Agatha noticed she could not completely understand so she did not write them down. She felt kind of helpless and she did not know who to call that would be able to help. She told them both to sit tight that she would be right back, she said she'd go look for help.

She dialed a number on her phone and she prayed that it would go through and not come out as white noise, when she heard the phone ringing she was well overjoyed. A woman picked up on the other end and once the situation was explained the woman said that she'd be right over to watch them.

After about an hour and a half of waiting the woman that Agatha talked to over the phone arrived. She got out of her Jeep

Grand Cherokee and walked up to the front door, knocked a few times and then went inside. The man and Benita were still sitting at the table rambling on about the same issues that they have been for the past hour, the woman noticed their eyes had not changed any colors, they were still crimson and bright white. She turned to Agatha and told her to go ahead and go that she would stay with them if she could, she would stay at least an hour. And with that said Agatha walked out the door and took off.

Agatha drove by rows of houses, some painted blue, yellow, red, but the majority were painted white just like hers. It bothered her a little and that she was not unique in her style of painting on her house, but at the same time she really didn't care. She thought about her home for a moment, thought about the fountain in the front yard and how every hour on the hour birds of every color and kind would flock to her fountain and her bird feeder, feed themselves and bathe themselves and then fly off. She thought about her statue of the Mother Mary, and how her statue showed the exposure of Mary's Sacred Heart. No one else around her had that statue.

Suddenly a white station wagon jerked out in front of her, causing Agatha to snap back into reality! She jerked the wheel left and right and slammed on the brakes doing everything she can not to hit the car in front of her. The Jeep came to a screeching stop, so did the white station wagon.

The driver got out. He seemed to have something in his hand and he walked towards the Jeep very slowly and methodically. Agatha had the doors already locked and all the windows up, and she had herself unbuckled and hidden in between the seats praying that the man did not see her.

Suddenly glass shattered and entered the vehicle and landed directly on her back, cutting into her neck and the back of her head. She screamed so loud and so terrified that she thought the man would've run away, but when she peeked her head up and looked out the driver side window she found herself with a gun pointed at her head…

CHAPTER 2

Dorian awoke the next morning after the "incident" and felt perfectly fine. He brushed his dark mahogany hair and got ready for the day. As he came out of his room, he noticed that there was a giant mess all over the place. It was something that he despised, but when he walked out into the living room aside from the shock of the mess, he noticed the muddy tracks along the floor and finally he heard the voices of people talking.

The people that were there were dressed in blue and black with stars on their covers, guns in their holsters and possibly more belonging to them. He saw them putting things in bags with EVIDENCE written on the label. He hollered at them but none of them noticed him. None of them glanced over at him, none of them heard him.

A new kind of fear overtook Dorian. The people, the trash, the tracks that they were making in the carpet, the fact that the floor was now covered in mud and filth, and to top it all off they could not even hear him, lead him to bang his hands against the wall in frustration.

He banged on the wall nearest him a couple of times when suddenly a voice came to him:

"There's no need to fret my PET. We must get you to a place of your own. Come to 401 Dragon Den Boulevard. It is the last apartment on the left. I know for a fact you'll love it. It has already been paid for. One year's rent in advance. Do not make me regret this,"

"Wow! For Master to do all of this, I can't believe him!" Dorian said aloud. Then a thought hit him, 'Why did I hear the Master's voice just now?' he wasn't sure how to explain it, nor did he care to. He was too deep into his own little world.

The next question that popped into his head was how to get to Dragon Den Boulevard. He didn't have to ponder on it long. Something popped up on the coffee table that seemed like it was only visible to him. It was gold-plated, and it had something attached to it but from the distance Dorian was at a loss as to what it was. He felt a little nervous trying to move towards the thing with everyone there.

Just as soon as that item showed up, the crowd of people began to disperse. He still sensed them on the property, but they were not inside, at least not all of them. When he got to the coffee table he noticed that the gold-plated item was not actually gold-plated, but gold!

Attached to this gold item, which was in the shape of a key, was a silver key ring that had a Dragon on it. When he pressed the button, gray smoke bellowed out from its mouth.

So, Dorian thought that this key was obviously for his apartment, but how was he to get there? And the other question that began to nag him even harder was why anyone could not see him nor hear him?

He went back into his room and noticed two men there, one at the foot of his bed and the other at the head. He heard a zipper close and watched as the two men slung a bagged object onto a gurney and then wheeled it out into the living room.

That's when he got the sense that something happened, that something happened to him. BUT WHAT??

Below the key was a note. Dorian opened the paper and read the note aloud:

> "Dear Dorian,
> Since the beginning we have watched over our own, and now that you are with us we expect great things from you.
> Your sacrifice has gone unnoticed, but Agatha has found herself in a very LIVELY situation. We'd like

for you to investigate her at your earliest convenience and stop her from doing such things.

We don't need her to stumble on anything that she does not need to discover.

Good luck, you're going to need it.

Signed,
The Order of the Light"

Dorian now had a good feeling about his situation. He felt that The Order of the Light put their faith in him and he was not going to let them down. He swore right then and there that he would find Agatha at any cost.

He found himself facing a new conundrum when he stepped outside. Officers, EMTs, and people from the city morgue were all standing around outside going over paperwork and scouring his front lawn. He realized that something was different about him, something obvious but not quite explained. He did not want to risk touching anyone. So, like a game of Tetris, he played like he was a game piece sliding through blocks of people trying to get to the bottom row.

He passed by a woman who was dressed in blue who did not have any identification on her, no star on her cover or her jacket but she was taking pictures of the scene. Dorian tried to inch behind her and found himself caught between her and his vehicle. Suddenly she stood up and she and Dorian merged as one being. For a moment or two Dorian knew all her thoughts, secrets, and everything about her. Those moments that he was inside her were terrifying for the woman, it was so severe that it took her breath away for a few minutes afterwards.

Dorian was frozen; he could not move. The woman did not sense him at all, though. Once she caught her breath and stood straight, she stepped away from that area and went to another where more tags were placed on the ground.

'What the heck was that?' Dorian thought nearly speaking out loud. Suddenly lights began flashing and a horn went off.

"Dorian come on man, we have places to go to,"

"Who's speaking?"

"Just get in, hurry up already,"

The bright lights faded and before Dorian was a Nissan Pathfinder. It was black as night and it looked like something Batman would use as a vehicle. It had a crimson strip along the side of it and when Dorian opened the door the inside was bright red and smelt fresh and clean. That new car smell.

"Come on Dorian!" said a woman in a pink coat and hat.

"Where are we going?" Dorian asked.

"Give me the key and I'll take you to Dragon Den Boulevard,"

"What key are you referring to? How do I know you're really here for me?"

"The one that The Order of the Light had given to you, just place it in my hand and we will be on our way,"

Dorian did just that. He took the key out of his pocket and pressed the dragons button one more time and watched the smoke come bellowing out of its mouth. He placed the key into the woman's hands and the woman in pink turned it to the right and the vehicle roared to life. It shook a handful of times like there was something particularly wrong with it and then she turned the vehicle and started to drive away from his house.

The woman in pink took the back roads veering left and right behind houses and sometimes cutting through them altogether. There were plenty of times when Dorian was screaming out but she kept it up, sometimes harder than before. Finally, she found the highway and turned left onto it and got up to full speed. Dorian looked at the speedometer and it read 120 miles an hour! Dorian's face paled and he nearly passed out.

"What's the matter Dorian, can't handle a little speed?" The woman in pink teased.

"I can handle a little speed, but the speed we're going is ridiculous!"

"Well, I was told to get you there as fast as I can. I'm doing just that,"

"Well you could've warned me you know. Is there anything else you're about to do that I should be warned about?"

"Yes, we are about to take flight, hang on to something," She said and just as she said that Dorian heard a popping sound coming from the sides of the vehicle. He looked out the driver side window and noticed flashing white lights on the left-hand side of the car.

Next thing Dorian knew there was a sudden jerking motion and Dorian was pulled back against the seat. He felt like his insides were going to be pulled out to his outsides and everything from there would be mismatched and splattered all over the vehicle. In fact, he even imagined this happening. He felt some bumps and his stomach jumped into his throat. The woman said something, but he didn't quite catch it.

Suddenly the flight leveled out and he felt fine, and he and the vehicle's driver, for a little while had a great conversation.

"We are nearly there Dorian, probably another three or four minutes and we'll be touching down get ready,"

"So, what is it that happened to me? Where am I going? What is this all about?"

"I'm not the one who should be answering those questions, if it isn't obvious to you now then it will be later. Your Master should be the one to answer those questions,"

Dorian bowed his head and thought about his Master who had been dead for years. 'How's my Master going to see me when he's been dead for so long?"

The Pathfinder gained altitude and began to experience turbulence. The shaking of the vehicle rattled Dorian and the sudden climb pushed him deeper into his seat. She laughed and mocked Dorian in his state of distress.

"What's the matter Dorian? Can't handle the air?"

"The air is fine when the pilot knows how to fly,"

They bickered back and forth like this for the remainder of the flight and before Dorian knew it they were touching down on asphalt.

"Welcome to your new home, Dorian. The key is in the glove box. Now, get out of MY car!"

Dorian scoffed and got out of the vehicle. He stumbled around to the passenger side, opened the door and retrieved the key from the glove compartment. He couldn't see much of his surroundings. There was barely any light around him. What he could see was a building that appeared to be gray in color and very long. He walked towards it and in the dim light he noticed on the key-chain there were numbers attached: 1472.

Under the dimly lit sky, Dorian found himself stumbling through the darkness looking for apartment number 1472. Everything looked the same. The gray walls, the beige doors and the hedges all blended together. It was difficult to tell anything apart, especially without a flashlight. Still Dorian continued to search. The door numbers were painted black, so Dorian had to squint at each door he approached to make out the numbers.

After another 10 minutes of searching he finally found the door. He put the key in the lock and turned it, but the door would not open.

"Why does this keep happening to me?"

"Have you tried pressing the button?", came a voice out of nowhere.

"Button? What button?", asked Dorian.

"You have not found the button yet? It puffs out smoke," The voice sounded old and a little shaky, like that of an elderly man.

Dorian fumbled with the key pulling it out of the lock and sliding his finger up and down the Dragon until he found the button. He saw a puff of green smoke come bellowing out of the Dragon's mouth. Suddenly he heard the click of the door unlocking, but when he turned to try the door it would not budge.

So, Dorian reinserted the key. Turning it left gave him a hard time and he nearly broke the key off. The door did not move at all. So, he tried the opposite direction and lo and behold the door opened wide and out poured a bright, white light. The light was so bright that Dorian had to wait a moment or two before entering the apartment. After his eyes had adjusted, Dorian stepped into the apartment and immediately noticed the glass chandelier hanging in the entryway that was the source of the bright light that nearly blinded him.

The apartment seemed empty and looked immaculate, as if no one had lived there before. The place was completely furnished. In the back-right corner of the living room, sat a large elaborately ornamented brown leather chair. A wooden bookcase that had been painted black ran along the back wall. It contained an extensive library of books ranging in subject matter from the occult to business practice. Directly in front of the bookcase lay a lion skin rug. To the left of the doorway, there were 2 black leather reclining love-seats and 1 royal purple microfiber sofa that were situated around a black and white area rug. In the center of this communal setup sat a glass coffee table with black legs and above it another chandelier, although much larger and more elaborately decorated than the first, adorned the ceiling.

Pictures of his Master, along with other members of his "Society", hung on the charcoal gray walls.

Dorian turned and spotted one large window in the wall to the left of him that was covered with purple drapes. He began to walk around the apartment and discovered a hallway on the left-hand side of the bookcase. He strode down the hallway, noticing doorways on the left and right leading into two medium sized bedrooms decorated in a way to match the tone of the living room. Dorian continued memorizing the floor plan as he walked. There were more pictures and a list of by-laws for the Society and one for The Order of Light hanging on the walls. He walked down another ten steps and turned left into another hallway. At the end of the hallway, there stood a large wooden door.

The upstairs was much like the downstairs, except that it housed the master bedroom as well as three skylights, one in the master bedroom, bathroom and the last one in the center of the hallway. He walked into the master bedroom and there he stopped. On the bed which again was covered in purple and black he found a note.

The front of the note said:

Do not open until morning but take two pills from the bottle and all will be remembered.

"What in the world could this be talking about?" Dorian said aloud.

"That is simple sir," Came a rather old shaky voice. Dorian recognized this voice from earlier and he dropped the note back on the bed and quickly turned around to see an old man staring back at him.

"You just gave me a start! I thought I heard voices over an intercom, but I wasn't quite sure. Is anybody else here?"

"Not at the moment sir," said the old man. Dorian now noticed that he was dressed up in a black and white suit with a little black bow-tie at the top, Dorian's first immediate thought was… Is he a Butler?

"Who are you sir?"

"I am your head Butler sir, I take care of things that need to be taken care of. I delegate duties that need to be handled properly. The rest of the staff will be here in the morning you can meet them then. In the meantime, sir, why don't you take your pills and get a good night's rest,"

"But I just got here, I would like to explore a little bit –,"

"I do apologize sir, if I lead you to believe that there was another way about this. There is only one option here, my way or Hell. You choose which you'd rather,"

Dorian hung his head low, took the pills and laid down. Dorian's sleep was restless, he tossed and turned all night.

Once the 12 stabbed Agatha, Dorian looked up at the sky, he watched the stars begin to dance and play. He watched as they (the 12) collected the blood into the gold chalices laced with rubies. 12 men drank the blood and mumbled something under their breaths. Dorian knew that their prayer was going to work tonight, he just felt it in his gut.

Suddenly the ground began to shake.

A couple of cracks began to form around the Altar.

Suddenly there was a loud snapping sound, like stone just broke in half! It was an eerie, terrifying, also one of the most peculiar sounds that Dorian had ever heard before. But it got all 13 men's attention. They watched as Agatha slid down between the cracks in the Altar and completely disappeared.

Dorian rushed to the Altar, but he was too late to save her body. But just as her body completely disappeared out of his sight he noticed something else crawling up. Dorian backed away quickly nearly falling over on to his back and scooting away like a crab, and surrounding them were hands that were popping up, followed by slight sounds of demonic laughter and screams, terrifying screams.

All 13 men were huddled together like a giant mass of cattle when this tall red and black being emerged from the ground. Dorian being the leader of this operation and being 6 feet 7 inches, was the tallest of them all, he was quickly selected to be the one to face this demonic being.

Dorian stepped up to this "creature" and with a brief look over noticed that it had two blackened horns like a bull, but instead of sticking out the side of his head they were sticking out of the front of his head. Outside of that he had a normal human looking face, this "creature" was extremely muscular and very well-toned, and when Dorian went down to his knee he noticed that the "creature's" legs were human as well. Outside of the horns and him being fully painted red there is nothing else demonic about him that Dorian could see.

"You 12," the demon snorted, "have failed me for the last time. You keep bringing me the wrong type of girl," The demon pulled out a Newport cigarette, and with a snap of his fingers he lit it. "This girl that you brought me, was the closest to being correct! For that, I shall only kill all of you mercifully instead of mercilessly,"

The demon looked down and noticed Dorian was still on his knees while the other 12 were still all cowering in a massive circle and shivering like little Chihuahuas. The demon noticed that Dorian was not.

"Are you not scared of death, son?"

Dorian just stayed in his kneeling place without moving, without saying a word. So, the demon asked once more, "Are you not scared of death, son?"

Dorian looked up at the demon, and with eyes that matched the demons, cold and calculating, he shook his head no and said that he was not afraid of death.

The demon began to laugh, deep and hard. He put his icy hand on top of Dorian's shoulder, which surprised Dorian, a demon with an icy hand. So, Dorian began to wonder how deep in hell this demon came from. Or exactly where this demon "really" came from.

The demon lifted Dorian off the ground and had him standing on both of his feet where he could look at him eye to eye.

"Turn and look Human, look at your rewards,"

The demon turned Dorian and he was made to watch as the other 12 members of his cult were each grabbed one by one, and pulled underneath the ground, removed from the Earthly surface that they're used to, only to suffer for eternity under the watchful gaze of their new "companion,"

Dorian wanted to cry out, scream, anything to let them know he was there and that he had feelings for them, that he was watching them suffer. But he was powerless to do so. That demon had a quite a hold on him, and he felt that there was nothing that he could do.

Dorian knew that his turn was next, so he closed his eyes and thought about Agatha. Thought about what they did to her and how he missed her.

"Don't worry Dorian," the demon began, "I have a special task for you, and a special place for you," with that said another demon rose up from the underworld and grabbed Dorian by his underarms and began to carry him off into the sky. Dorian flew high, higher than the trees, then suddenly the demon released Dorian!

Dorian started flailing his arms like a bird, he was screaming all the way down. The demon that was in human form stood by the Altar nearest Dorian's body, and he reached down picked up Dorian's battered remains and handed them to the demon that was flying and told him to take them to Dorian's house and lay them on his bed. He said that the Society paid big money for him to "collect" Dorian and bring him to Nebula. The two demons began laughing and then they faded from existence on the Earthly plane.

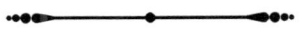

Dorian stretched his arms and yawned, threw back the covers and stepped out of bed. There was a note on the mirror at the dresser which was at the foot of his bed;

> "Dorian,
> Downstairs you will find that everything is in order and the staff has arrived. The Order of Light has spared no expense in providing you with the very best.
> The chef will cook you whatever you ask for, I recommend the steak.
> When you are done, my servant will take care of things until I return. Please listen to him as you have listened to me and don't give him a hard time."

Dorian found his clothing inside the drawers of the dresser in front of him, so without wasting another moment Dorian got dressed. He put on a pair of blue jeans with the dark blue T-shirt. On the shirt, there was a design of two wolves and lightning connecting them in the center.

Once he was finished dressing, he walked out the door and down the stairs to the tall wooden door at the end of the hallway, opened the door and stepped out. He stepped down the hallway a little bit turned right and passed the hallway full of photos of past members and current members of the Society and of The Order of the Light as well as the bylaws from both organizations.

He made his way up into the living room and noticed a few people scurrying about dusting, vacuuming and straightening. One person was straightening up the couch and sofas, while another person was straightening up the books in the bookcase. Both of those gentlemen were in red and black matching uniforms and they had what looked like a red golfers style hat on their heads. The glass coffee table was moved off the area rug and there was a lady in matching uniform vacuuming it. She had headphones on her head and her chocolate brown hair was tied up into a bun. She had glasses on her face and freckles all over her nose, Dorian thought she was kind of cute in the face at least a side view of it.

As he stepped out of the hallway everyone stopped doing what they were doing and bowed to him. Dorian smiled, return the bow and once he was back standing straight up asked them where you can go to get a bite to eat. The lady that was vacuuming gave the whole come here motion with her hand and as soon as Dorian was over there she turned Dorian, so that he could see this for himself.

So, Dorian walked up, and something caught his eye on the right-hand side of the wall. It was a hallway, a hallway that was not there the day before. To Dorian's recollection, there was nothing but a bunch of pictures covering the wall, no hallway, but now there was one.

Dorian looked over at the lady that was vacuuming, and she pointed and nodded, and he walked down the hallway.

Pictures lined the dark hallway, even though it was daylight outside the hallway seemed to have a dark aura about it. Dorian could make out all the pictures, he stopped and stared at a Colonel with a brown mustache on his face, across from the Col. was another picture of a woman in black with a white umbrella. Continuing his way down there were children in some of the pictures as well.

The hallway came to an end and it opened into this wide elaborate dining hall, in the center was a long wooden table with matching stools along the side of it and a chandelier hanging in the center. To the left of the table and nearest the entrance-way, as Dorian discovered when he rounded the corner, there was a large fireplace. It had a stone wall the back that was charred from all the burning, a metal rack in the center where the wood was placed, outside of it the stone looked smooth, polished and it was speckled with multicolored stones.

On top of the mantel were chalices from various ages. And in the center, was his picture. Dorian nearly dropped his photo on the floor when he realized that it was a photo of himself that he was looking at.

On the left-hand side of the room, with Dorian facing the table, were three large windows. They went from floor to ceiling and the ceiling had to be nearly 12 to 15 feet in height.

'What's up with this place? For an apartment, this place is elaborate it's like a castle.' Dorian thought.

Suddenly a man appeared in front of him and bowed. The man was dressed in red and black (which seemed to be the uniform of the house) and guided Dorian to his seat at the head of the table. He was handed a menu and the man that lead him there just stood there like he was waiting for something.

Dorian tried speaking but he wasn't sure what to say. The man pointed at the menu and pointed closer to the breakfast section where he touched the steak and eggs, then he gave Dorian the big thumbs up. Dorian nodded and said that he would take it, the man in red and black grabbed the menu and walked into the back room through the double doors and came back out a few minutes later with a glass of water and a bottle of wine in the other hand.

The man sat the bottle of wine down in front of Dorian, followed by the glass of water. Then like magic the man clapped his hands twice and a cupboard rolled out with a wineglass on it and a bucket of ice, as well as a rolled-up napkin with a knife and fork inside of it. The man put some ice cubes in Dorian's wineglass and poured in the red wine. Now Dorian liked red wine, but he never had it for breakfast it was usually with Italian meals.

Next thing Dorian knew the man was carrying back his steak and eggs. The man nodded and patted Dorian on the back once more gave him the thumbs up and motioned for Dorian to eat. So, Dorian picked up the knife and fork, and he cut into the steak that looked just right.

His taste buds soared with the juices and sensation that he felt with the very first bite of that steak. It was like an attack on his taste buds an attack that needed repeating and more repeating until the plate was empty.

The man in red and black had been standing by the entire time waiting for Dorian to finish eating, and when he was done eating and drinking he came over and took Dorian's plate and cups. Dorian tried to say that he would help but the man just shook his head.

Dorian rose from the table, turned and double checked the stool that he was sitting on and said, "Wow this thing is quite comfy,"

"Yes, they are Master," came a familiar voice from Dorian's past.

Dorian then smelled a very familiar scent, but he couldn't quite place it. It was a smell of lavender. He remembered smelling it from his earlier days, but he couldn't remember from when.

"Master, it's been a while hasn't it," The woman came into the room dressed in purple and black. It was a beautiful dress, it wasn't the normally striped dress that he usually sees on women, this one seemed a bit more businesslike. Thick heavy stripes of purple in between black ones wrapping around her slender body, with her long flowing blonde hair just tied up in a ponytail and left to dangle. She wore purple and black high heeled shoes that clinked on the ground as she walked. She made her way over to Dorian. As she got closer to him she bowed and as she rose Dorian embraced her and she stood up higher and kissed him on his cheek.

"What is your bidding, Master?" She said rubbing her sides and placing her hands on her hips.

"What's with this Master business? You know as well as I do I'm not the Master Veronica,"

"Well that's not the memo that we all got. You might want to talk to your Butler," Veronica stated with a matter-of-fact tone. Dorian stared deep into her sea green eyes and imagined himself being lost out at sea in them, sailing for days without a drop of water and that's when he came to his senses.

They started playing catch-up for a few minutes, when Dorian realized that he had no idea why he or she was there, he received a letter at his house telling him to be here and he came. So, he explained his situation to her and she had a similar situation as well; it turns out that Veronica was part of The Order of the Light and she too oversaw her area as well, over the course of three or four years she sacrificed some 15, 16 people, a good mixture of both men and women, until she found what she thought was the perfect candidate. On the same full moon night that she was inducted, she sacrificed this man and when the demon rose it swallowed all her disciple's whole and they murdered her.

"I wonder what they want us for?" Dorian asked.

"I'm not sure, all that I know is that you're in charge. For the moment anyway,"

Just then a man came in, wearing red and black again and now Dorian knew that this was a uniform for sure, carrying a piece of paper and a telephone.

"Sir, your Butler told me to bring you this after you ate," he handed the platters over to Veronica and she held them out for Dorian who stared at the parchment.

> "Dorian,
> The time has come for me to inform you that Agatha is here with us in Nebula. She can 'Channel' humans.
> Call her at the number below and tell her that you need her. I'm on my way to get her for you.
> Some convincing, after all, you're Boss, Master,"

Dorian picked up the red telephone and dialed the number and left a message. Veronica had thought that the message he left was a little too personal, but she wasn't going to say anything against the Masters wishes. There was a slight pain in Veronica's heart when she heard Dorian tell Agatha's answering machine that he loved her, for no one has ever told her that, not the way he just told her that.

Once Dorian hung up the phone, Veronica placed both platters in the servant's hands and grabbed Dorian and tried to swing him around, but he did not budge.

"What are you trying to do?"

"Twirl you, you know spinning around like we did when we were younger,"

"That was a long time ago Veronica, long before The Order of the Light,"

Suddenly a man burst into the room, he was in a long black robe with white dragons laced around the bottom. He was tall, dark-haired, pale skinned with dark brown eyes with just a hint of gold shimmering all around them, he had a book in one hand and a jacket in the other.

The closer he came, the stranger the feeling Dorian received. It was like Dorian was afraid of him, but he didn't know why.

The man with the dragon robe dropped his jacket revealing his secret.

In his left hand was a pistol, and as soon as he got in front of Dorian, he pointed it straight at Veronica's head. He looked over at Dorian and smiled. It was a terrifying smile, Dorian had one of those once before, but this is the first time he has ever seen one close-up, Dorian did not know what to do.

"Master…" The man snarled and pulled back the hammer, "If you don't want her to fade into nothingness, then you better do exactly as I say,"

There came a sudden scream in the background and the gunman pulled the trigger!

Chapter 3

"You're coming with me Agatha," said the Gunman.

"Yes, of course," Agatha said knowing if she said anything else the Gunman could possibly shoot her. She got out of the Jeep and closed the door. She took a couple steps away from the Jeep watching the Gunman the entire time.

"Good, now get into this car," the Gunman pointed to a white Honda Accord, the car was parked just on the other side of his. Agatha could hear the car's engine running, she could see the smoke bellowing out of the tailpipe. The walk there was long and distressing, full of pain and misery, Agatha's knees buckled, and she felt that her feet were starting to drag, and this worried her. The next thing that she knew the sound of the gun went off which made her jump back a great distance.

"Come on! It's not far and don't keep the Master waiting!" The Gunman shouted at her in a very commanding voice. Agatha wanted to shout back at him, but she was too afraid of being struck by a bullet somewhere, so she regrouped and re-gathered her strength kept herself quiet and made her way into the car.

Once she made it into the car and the gunman closed the door behind her, she could not believe who was in there waiting for her!

"Surprised aren't you Agatha, I knew you would be. I've taken the luxury of making sure that vehicle behind this gets completely repaired and sent back to your house.

"The two visitors there will be brought over to our home. There they will be studied and kept under lock and key until we can figure out what is going on. I had told you before Agatha, we needed your help. You did not take the offer one way, so I had to give you the offer another way.

"Would you like some champagne?" Asked the man in the blue uniform. Something seemed off about him to Agatha, he seemed a bit out of place. He was of average height with an average build and he was an older gentleman with salt and pepper hair. He had this presence about him that he oversaw something huge, that he was a great deal, a huge person of some sort. He gave off a huge tone of authority in other words and he commanded respect especially when he was face-to-face with you.

Agatha felt kind of tiny in retrospect for what she did earlier to him, especially with this new feeling now.

"No, no, no, no, thank you. And I'm sorry for earlier. But I have a lot going on in my own daily life,"

"I can understand that Agatha," he began while pouring a glass of champagne for himself, "but my master assures me that you are the right person for this task, and he is rarely wrong,"

"What's this task?"

"Todd, go ahead and go home, she'll be fine with us," the old man said, then turning his attention back to Agatha, "I can best explain at the house. Please keep an open mind and eye,"

The white Honda Accord rolled down the road with little resistance, there was no traffic to speak of, no lights to worry about (for they were all green), lastly, no one was out and about. It was likely everyone was inside hiding from the gunfire that just erupted not that far from them.

Agatha and the old man had light conversations on their way to the house, talking of the weather and of the time. When the car came to a stop, Todd got out of the car and opened Agatha's side first, he led her to the sidewalk and told her to wait there. Todd went to the other side and opened the door for the old man.

When the old man came out of the car and appeared on the sidewalk, Agatha had a sigh of relief come over her. The old man did not appear as tall as the way that his presence gave off that he was. The old man walked up to her with power in his steps, and she thought that he was still powerful and spry for an old man.

"Welcome to your new home Miss Agatha," the old man bowed and raised his left arm pointing towards the house. She turned and looked and what she saw her little white house was far more appealing. This place looked like a run-down haunted mansion, with all its doors and windows rusted or on the verge of falling off, the only color that was on the house was on the door and its numbers, which were red and black respectfully.

And those doors and numbers were multiple all over the area. Agatha counted 10 of them.

"Come with me Agatha, don't let appearances fool you,"

Agatha took several steps towards the old man and the old man stretched out his hand and grabbed hers and led her through the opening steps. She passed through an archway that seemed to have some scratch marks that looked fresh. As soon as she crossed through the archway the sun had disappeared and darkness overtook all. Agatha didn't scream or squeal, but she did cling tighter to the old man who only shook his head.

"It does this with all new people. Please forgive our traditions," Agatha nodded her head.

The old man, knowing where he was going led Agatha, who could not see an inch in front of her nose. She tried waving her hand in front of her face and she couldn't see it. But when the old man stopped moving, he tugged on her as she tried to continue, she turned and came to a stop as well.

The old man pressed a button and Agatha caught a hint of green smoke pop out of something, then he opened the door and a bright shock of daylight overtook her eyes.

"God can this day be any brighter?" she complained loudly, not meaning to, but she did.

"Yes, it can,"

"Huh?"

"I was answering your question; can the sun get any brighter? I said, it can,"

"Oh…sorry, I didn't mean to say that out loud,"

Just then a woman in red and black passed behind the old man and he stopped her and whispered something in her ear and the woman turned around and took off the other way.

"It's fine my dear, we all make mistakes from time to time. Come, I want to show you something," the old man held out his hand and Agatha took it and he led her across the room and through two doors where she was exposed to a scene that she least expected.

"Master...," said a man in a black looking robe with what looked to be white dragons circling around the bottom of it. He seemed to be holding something, but Agatha could not tell what it was at the distance she was at.

The old man motioned for her to stay silent and he silently approached.

She crept along from the other side trying not to make much of a commotion, but rather hide in plain sight. There were a couple of red and black drapes that hung down to the floor about 10 feet from where she stood, so she slunk her way over to them and tried her best to be stealthy and hide behind them.

Agatha saw the man with the dragon robe hold out a weapon in his left hand and he was pointing it at some woman who stood next to Dorian in a purple and black striped dress. She looked terrified and at the same time she didn't recoil or make a movement. Agatha thought this woman brave in this much danger. So, Agatha took it upon herself to attack the man from the side without the fear of a final and permanent death.

Running across the floor she ran as fast and as hard as she could, she leaped in the air towards the man in the dragon robe and inadvertently released a loud scream when she wanted to be as silent as possible. The man turned his attention towards her and fired off a round from his pistol.

Agatha dropped like a rock out of the air and fell hard onto the ground making a loud thud. Dorian and Veronica just stared at the man and then at the body of Agatha. They seemed to be waiting for her to get up or do anything. They were more in a shock that something like this COULD and DID happen to them, right in front of them.

"Master..." the gunman's voice was straining some, "Master, I want... arrrrgh!" the man's weapon fell from his hands and Dorian quickly ran up and kicked it away. For the next few seconds Dorian and Veronica watched as the gunman transformed.

The gunman began a change, his body began to convulse, without stopping, white foam began pouring out from the sides of his mouth and blood poured out from his ears and nose. He arched his back and his neck seemed to pop in several places. He turned his head around and stared off at the floor for a moment. He then turned his sideways head towards the two of them and Dorian and Veronica took a few steps back.

His body began to mutate. His head shook violently and was spinning in a near 360 degrees, his arms and legs stretched out wide and stood long like someone doing the warrior pose in yoga. They heard no yelling, no screaming, no sound of any kind from this man.

Once it stopped, Dorian saw a man with wide eyes – red, crimson in color with a demonic white in the center–he started mumbling words, some were incoherent, others were able to be understood.

"Church, stabbing, new God, Christ child worship, pigs, cats, Rape of Eve,"

Just as soon as Dorian got that little bit figured out, men in black and red suits came and grabbed a hold of him and began walking him off.

One of the men looked down at Agatha and pointed and was told to do nothing with or for her.

They took the man with the dragon robe somewhere unknown.

Dorian and Veronica rushed over to Agatha's body and rolled her over onto her back. Dorian quickly realized Agatha was not breathing, and he began to do compressions. He told Veronica to breathe after every 10 pumps of his hands. Together Dorian and Veronica worked on bringing Agatha back to life.

"Come on Aggie!" Dorian cried after a minute of pumping. "Please Agatha, please come back to us," Veronica said teary eyed.

They were just about to give up when the old man showed up, "Sir, if I may take over for you. I have brought a machine that should help us. You hook it up while I pump,"

The machine was white, it had three buttons on it and two paddles on either side. On the left side Dorian noticed these things that looked like band-aids, and on the right, was some green goo in a bottle. Dorian wheeled it over towards Agatha and followed the instructions on hooking it up. Then he turned on the charging unit and waited until it was charged and put some goop on it and told the old man and Veronica that it was ready.

Agatha's body arched with the electrical current that flowed through it, then it landed just as quick. It was as fast as 3 or 4 heartbeats and Agatha still laid there not breathing.

The old man snapped his fingers and two men in white suits came rushing in and placed her on the gurney they were carrying. Dorian started to chase after them so that he knew where she was going but the old man put a stop to it.

"Sir, if I may, you have more important things to take care of here.

Veronica and I shall go and attend to the girl,"

"I understand," Dorian said feeling sorrowful.

Veronica walked up and kissed his cheek and told him that she'd be back with news. Then the two of them left and Dorian was finally alone.

DAY 1 (A few hours later):

"Sir, a note just came in for you, shall I read it?" said one of the people in the red and black outfits.

"Be my guest,"

"Yes sir," she cleared her throat, "Dorian, there is an abundant amount of work to be done. Look into the cause of the redeyed people. Agatha's doing better, she's coming around and should make a full recovery in a matter of days... Don't be so hard on yourself.

"That's all it says sir,"

"Thank you...um...,"

"We have no names here sir. Those of us in red and black have no names. And if we do, it's because our master has given us one,"

"Why is that?" Dorian asked with sheer curiosity.

"Do you wish to own me sir?"

Dorian took his time looking this sweet young lady over, she had red hair that was tied up in a bun, an average build (curves were not a problem for Dorian), her voice was soothing, like a bell. She had a broad face and a nose that seemed a little wider than normal, but what entrances Dorian the most are her sky-blue eyes. Looking into them like how he was while she was reading his letter was like flying like a bird in a never-ending sky.

"No, not now anyway...can you just answer my question?"

"Of course, when a master owns one of us, he or she can do whatever they want. From beatings for pleasure to a romantic relationship. When a master picks us, they give us a name. Any name that they want. I know a man that was named Hose and another named Fire. They ended up being used for unmentionable experiments and situations, but they're gone now. I hope they're in a better place,"

"I'm sorry to hear about your friends. But you're telling me that if I owned you, you'd be mine, mind, body, soul, anything and everything? Is that what I understand?"

"Yes,"

"First off, who sent you to me?"

"I'm sorry sir?"

"You heard me,"

"I'm afraid I don't understand the question,"

"Did anyone send you to me or did you come up here to me on your own?"

"On my own, why?"

"Fine. I may ask more questions later. But for now, I'd like for you to stay by my side and not to leave it,"

The red hair girl was jumping up and down for joy, she could not believe she was getting chosen.

"I'm not picking you just yet, but I don't want to lose you either. Stay by my side and you may have a master by the nights end. And a name,"

The excitement swelled inside her and before she could let out a scream, Dorian placed his hand over her mouth and shook his head.

"You need to calm down girl," Dorian said softly.

The girl nodded her head, "I'll do my best sir, it's just that I have never been given this opportunity before,"

"Well then this is a first for both of us,"

She tried to jump inside Dorian's arms and wrap hers around his neck, but Dorian would not have it. He reminded her that he said she had to calm down and relax, she apologized and began to leave the room. Dorian followed right behind her.

"So, tell me girl, what do you know of these redeyed people?"

"I know absolutely nothing sir," she said while shaking her head. They walked down the hall and into the living room. There were four people working, one was dusting, another was vacuuming, one was organizing the bookshelves, and the last one stood by the door and waited for something or someone. The redheaded girl grabbed hold of Dorian's hand led him into what looked like a ballroom. There were five people behind different instruments ready to play at a moment's notice.

"Do you know how to dance sir?" She asked while grabbing a hold of his hand and waist.

"I do, and apparently you wish to dance with me,"

The redheaded girl nodded, and the band began to play. Dorian led the way dancing a few steps here and there trying to get his footing, he stumbled a few times and she giggled not loudly but she giggled.

"It's not funny!"

"No sir, it is extremely cute. Which is why I giggled,"

The band started to slow down a bit, and they seemed to be playing a very soft love song. The redheaded girl and Dorian inched closer together until their bodies were touching. She stepped on the top of his feet, he was about to say something but decided against it, she laid her head on his chest and she closed her eyes and they swayed back and forth to the music.

"This is nice sir," she said and rubbed his back and side.

"It is, if there is only some way I could repay you for this kindness. I think I have an idea on how to do that though,"

The redheaded girl smiled a huge smile. Dorian knew there was no way to escape her, or the feelings that were growing for her. So, he might as well be her master. It was what she wanted after all.

So, Dorian thought hard for a few minutes while dancing with her this final song, then it hit him like a ton of bricks, her name just popped out of nowhere and hit hard.

By this time there was a large crowd of people gathering around Dorian and the redheaded girl and neither one of them seemed to notice it, Dorian asked the redheaded girl if there was a special ritual or something for him to ask her to be his and she told him to just ask the question.

Dorian looked around and noticed the people and he was about to say something, then he thought that witnesses were not always a bad thing.

"Redheaded girl, um… I'd like to be your master… If you'd… Take me for yours,"

The hall erupted in loud cheers, people were whistling, some were hooting and hollering, others were crying. The redheaded girl clung tightly to Dorian and said yes, she would be his for all eternity.

"Good, I am very pleased to hear that. Now all that's left is to give you a name is that right?"

"Yes, that's right,"

"Then your name shall be Catherine,"

Catherine was overjoyed at this, she finally had a name, after all those years of never being selected for anything she was finally chosen and now she had a name.

Catherine and Dorian did one more lap around the dance floor and everyone that was in there cheered louder than before, Dorian felt a smile come over his face. Catherine took that as a good sign and once the music stopped they stopped and the crowd dispersed.

"Now about your tasks for the day sir,"

"Yes,"

'Here," and Catherine handed the agenda over to Dorian who studied it carefully.

The agenda that he looked over had his day planned out to the second nearly, he noticed that it even had the time he was to sleep.

"Agatha, there's no slot on here for me to see her, why?"

"I'm not sure,"

"Hmm, interesting," he said and rubbed his chin, "we'll have to see how this day goes, so what's first?"

"Research Department. You need to talk to the Head of the Research Department about this growing epidemic,"

"Lead the way,"

Catherine grabbed a hold of Dorian's hand and led him up the stairs and once they were in his room Catherine laid out an outfit and pulled out a pair of size 10 and a half shoes. The outfit as Dorian looked at it was black and blue, a deep blue, and his undershirt was a bright white. His shoes were a black dress shoe and they looked fancy, a little too fancy for Dorian.

He started to take off his clothes when he remembered that Catherine was in the room staring at him with a wide-open faced smile.

"Do you have to be in here with me while I change as well?" Dorian asked a little annoyed.

"Yes, I do. I have to make sure that it fits all of you perfectly," her smile faded slightly since she noticed that it bothered Dorian some, she then stated that she would step outside for a few moments to let him take care of his pants issue and then she'd be back inside the room.

Once she was out of the room Dorian slipped out of his current pants and into the dress pants which surprisingly fit perfectly. He called upon Catherine and she opened the door to his room like it was her own.

She swept a piece of hair out of her face and wrapped it around her ear, she then walked around Dorian checking him out. She pulled on the pants from behind and from below, and then she made a comment; "Wow, perfect fit! I got it right on the first try,"

By this time Dorian had his white undershirt and his blue and black dress shirt on and tucked in. Once he finished buttoning it he turned and faced his new favorite redhead.

"How do I look?"

"You look fantastic Master!" Catherine said excitedly.

"You don't have to call me Master, you know,"

"You'd rather me call you Dorian?"

"Yes, it's bad enough that most the people here are doing it, as well as people that I know. I don't need you doing it as well,"

"As you wish Dorian,"

Catherine smiled at Dorian and then reminded him that they need to go to the Research Department. Soon the two of them were off down the stairs and out the door.

After about 5 or so minutes Dorian and Catherine emerged from the hallway and made their way to the front door, with Catherine leading Dorian much of the way. Dorian would periodically look at her and laugh in his head about how he can lead himself through the house and out to the car, but at this stage in the game, why bother.

They made it out the door and under the archway in a matter of moments, so it seemed. Dorian was blown away on how ragged the place looked on the outside versus how glamorous it was on the inside.

"You know," Dorian began pointing back at the house, "it looks a lot different at night,"

"I'm sure it does," Catherine said.

They reached the bottom of the sidewalk and Catherine began tapping her foot impatiently.

"Catherine, what's the matter, we just got here. Give the driver a moment or two,"

Catherine tried smiling at Dorian and tried to listen to him as well but wasn't happy that her Master was being kept waiting. About five minutes later a white car pulled up and a man in a blue suit got out and began apologizing like crazy. After a lecture on punctuality from Catherine, Dorian andCatherine loaded up and began their journey towards the Research Department, where hopefully they would find an answer for the sudden disturbance that nearly killed Dorian and put Agatha into the hospital.

Dorian and Catherine pulled up to an old red brick looking building that may have been used as a bomb making factory back in the 1940s. "Wow, what a sight!" Dorian exclaimed.

"I agree!"

"I believe that's the building you're looking for," the driver said pointing to a small white building about the size of a dome-shed with 4 of them attached to the sides for length.

"Oh, thank you, I guess," Dorian said.

Dorian was just about to begin to cross the road when Catherine screamed.

Agatha's body was tortured by the constant pain she was in. her ragged little body couldn't handle too much more, or so she thought.

It was at this point she started seeing them, a glitter, a glimpse, fragments of a picture...but what? What could they be?

Then she was back at the "apartment" and Dorian and some young lady had a guy in front of them with a gun pointed at them…

"Dorian!"

"Easy now Agatha," the old man said calmly, "you have just been through a very tragic event. Don't over exert yourself,"

As Agatha finished sitting up, she felt a pain in her left breast and arm.

"They'll hurt for a while. The doctors took out the bullet. Now rest, relax some Agatha,"

"But I don't even know what to call you, what's your name?"

"No one has asked me that in a while, my name is Jackson, but people call me Jack for short. It is a pleasure to meet your acquaintance Miss Agatha,"

"Well Jack, not the name I pitted for you," and Agatha began laughing until she hurt herself.

"Funny," Jack commented.

"How long am I looking to be here?"

"Waiting on the doc, she'll have the answer to that,"

After about what seemed like an hour or two, a lady in a blue dress walked into the room followed by two other nurses and they stood on either side of Agatha, as the blue dress lady stood at the end of the bed.

Agatha didn't really look at her, but more at the room, which was adorned with all sorts of monuments and flowers from all over the world and from many different eras. Agatha couldn't know or count them all.

To the left of her bed was what looked like a statue of Shiva and Buddha dipped in gold and placed there with care. They sat upon a red velvet tapestry and it too had gold leaf print.

To Agatha's right there was a Gladius and a Roman shield, it was red, with yellow wings coming out on the sides of the shield painting, with white lightning bolts touching those same wings.

All around the room Agatha took notice of various items from history scattered about. When Agatha's eyes met with the woman in front of her, Agatha took a hard gulp.

"Miss Agatha,"

"Yes ma'am,"

"It appears as though you are beginning to feel a bit better. I have news for you. The wounds appear to be superficial and you'll be fine by the end of the day,"

"So, does that mean I can leave? Am I being discharged?"

"Yes. My nurse will be back in here in a few minutes with the paperwork and instructions,"

The three of them left the room and closed the door behind them.

Agatha and Jack sat there, Agatha a little too excited for words, so Jack rose to his feet and began to sit on the edge of the bed. He grabbed a hold of her right hand and raised it to his lips and kissed it gently and said to her that he was going to get the car ready and that he'd be right back.

Once he was gone and Agatha was all alone, a nurse in blue scrubs walked into the room with a group of papers in one hand and a syringe in the other.

"What's the needle for?"

She didn't say anything; the nurse came in and placed everything down on the counter top and pulled out a few paper towels. She then placed the syringe on the towel and pulled out a vile of liquid from her pocket. The nurse held the tiny bottle up to the light stuck the needle into the end and drew out the liquid. The nurse turned and with a smile on her face, she began to walk towards Agatha.

Chapter 4

Veronica was in an extremely unpleasant situation, she was stuck having tea with a couple whose son always wore a black robe with dragons around it. But the grieving family wasn't mourning the loss of their son (who disappeared really), but the sudden claim of the grandmother. She seemed to be the head of the family and she kept them all in line and close.

"What do you mean by loss?" Veronica asked moving some of her blonde hair out of her face.

"Well Miss, we all went to sleep last night and early this morning there was a bright light," the woman in the red and blue floral dress said, she picked up a handkerchief off her lap and dried her eyes with it.

"And I says, 'We's got ourselves a UFO!'" the man in overalls stated without waiting a moment to spare.

"Yes, my dear, but then the light shone brightly into my mother's bedroom and we watched as she floated upwards and disappeared," she dried the few tears that fell once more.

Veronica wasn't sure what to do. She was not qualified to give these people therapy, but she was also not supposed to reveal the truth behind the veil either, even though she was thinking about it. Just to ease their suffering. Instead she has an idea, she looks at the two of them and takes another sip of her ice tea and then sets it down on the table beside her says, "I understand, I think anyway, your Mom, was taken last night by a strange white light and out of everyone here, you two are the only ones to see this. Correct?"

"Correct-ish," says the woman in the floral dress. "Whatcha gettin at?" asks the man in overalls.

"I believe that it was aliens, or a dream perhaps. A very wide spread dream, but who knows what can happen,"

"So how do we get her back?" Asked the woman.

"That's what I'm not sure about yet," Veronica took another sip of iced tea and snapped her fingers. Once the cup was down and she swallowed the liquid she told them to gather everyone over that knows about the event.

She watched as the two of them walked over from section to section collecting people, there were people from all sorts of ages and years old. They brought one man who seemed to be from the Egyptian Empire, another one was Roman, then one was Persian, one claimed to be Saxon, she found that this family had a whole horde from all over.

They were still talking to people and bringing them up one by one when Veronica just asked them to gather everyone and she'd go over this once. Slowly people emerged from their various styles of homes, some were houses and others were huts. Some had one person, others had up to 8 people in them and they were all different shapes and sizes. They all mad their way to Veronica, each taking a seat or standing underneath a nearby tree.

Veronica went to her car and pulled out a projector and a computer. She then went back to the group and grabbed a couple of the tallest men and had them grab a white cloth and hang it over the tree limb. Veronica then began her show. Lights began to flash before everyone's eyes, streams of reds, greens, blues and blacks. Then they just looked like they forgot what was happening and why Veronica was there.

"So, as you all can see. Grandma, the matriarch, simply went out for a long-spirited walk and we're not sure when she'll return,"

Veronica packed up and loaded up into her car and drove off. Once she got onto the paved road and received signal on her cell phone, she called the usual number to report in.

"This is Veronica, issues 1176-48 has been cleared and ready for evaluation,"

"Good, come on back and get ready, a new issue has arisen. I cannot explain over the phone, but when we meet tonight I shall," said the voice on the other end.

Veronica hung up the line and drove back to the "apartment" where she met up with the second in command, a mute gentleman named Geoffrey. She got out of the 2016 Chevy Cavalier and just looked at its destruction. The once beautiful candy-apple red car was now covered in dirt and mud. You could see the roof was red, but the rest was caked in mud and dirt and other stuck on debris.

A few of the outside gardeners came over dressed in their red and black uniformed overalls and began the fun task of cleaning her car.

Apparently, they didn't mind, the gardeners collected some of the dirt as a sample and the mud they threw at each other.

"Well, at least they're enjoying it. Now that I've seen it, I'm not happy about it," Veronica said under her breath as she walked into the apartment.

A little way in there sat a man in the far-right corner in the ornate chair, "Ah, you must be the infamous Veronica that I've heard so much about. Come, come, sit with me," said a man in a Hawaiian shirt and a pair of khaki pants. He had on a pair of New Balance tennis shoes, the purple and green pair, they seemed to glow, and it was very distracting. The man was rather large, not just in size, but with the way he carried himself he appeared to be a very important gentleman.

"So, what is it that I can do for you sir?" Veronica said while sitting down on the black love-seat closest to the door. The man in the Hawaiian shirt sat across from her and leaned forward placing his forearms on his knees and clasping his hands together replied, "A lot,"

"What do you mean sir? If you're here for any naughty purpose, then you can leave now. Otherwise state your business and we'll go from there,"

"You do have the tongue that I was told you'd have. Good to see it.

We are waiting for the third member of this conversation who should be arriving soon with a woman who is able to speak to the LIVING, or so I'm told,"

Veronica had a flash of two people the old man and Agatha. She wished that she knew the old man's name, but she was never given that privilege. But what did Agatha have to do with this?

She saw a shadow or two passed on the wall and it startled her a little.

Suddenly the door opened and in walked Agatha and the old man. "Sir, Agatha! You both look great. Nice to see you,"

"Ah, Veronica, happy you're here, this is the next assignment. Allow me to introduce case number 1175-75, remember, no names and no funny stuff," the old man said.

"So, Jack, is this whom you were telling me that needed my assistance?" Agatha asked.

"Yes, it is Agatha, and this is Veronica,"

"Pleased to meet you," Veronica said, "So what is it that we need her for?"

"Sit down and let us all discuss this and if I am forgetting anything then the Client, here sir, he can fill in the blanks," Jack said, and he and Agatha walked to the purple couch and sat down on opposite ends.

The temperature in the room seemed to increase with each passing moment and no one was speaking. Veronica was thrilled that she learned that Jack was the old man's first name and looked forward to learning more about him, Agatha was tickled pink that she was needed by someone other than her usual clients (which were her neighbors). The client sat there thinking about how to address the women if the man in the corner near him could not.

"Ladies-,"

A sudden blast rocked the building and the area around it shook violently. It was like an earthquake but worse than a 10 pointer. The roof of the building began to crumble and everything you could imagine came tumbling down on top of them, concrete slabs thick and heavy came crashing down and one nearly squished the client. Rubble of all sorts, wires, sinks, tubs, mirrors, shattered glass, everything you could imagine and more came crumbling inward. They barely made it out into the courtyard.

They did a body check on the group and seen that everyone was there, Jack then walked over to one of the uniformed people and said something and they too began counting heads.

"Jack," Veronica began, "what just happened?"

"You know, outside of the destruction, I'm not sure. I'm going to find out though," he said with purpose.

Agatha stood back and suddenly something came over her, her arms flew out to the side and she began moaning in different octaves, her head fell backwards and then her back soon followed.

"What in the world? Agatha, what is wrong with you?" Veronica questioned sharply.

"Quiet, I think she's channeling something? Let's take a listen," said the man in the Hawaiian shirt.

In the back-bend Agatha turned her head to face her comrades and opened her mouth and this gooey ooze came dripping out. It was slime green with a hint of red and it looked disgusting coming from such a beautiful young lady. She spat the goo towards them and it landed at their feet and she laughed at Veronica when she jumped back to avoid getting hit by the mess the laugh was a deep dark gurgling guttural sound, whirling around with an oozy mix...suddenly she rose to her feet the laughter gone, ooze gone, everything back to normal.

"Agatha?" Jack questioned her, "Are you there?"

Agatha reached out a hand for Jack and he grabbed it and immediately regretted it, he felt a grip the far surpassed anything any human (spirit or not) could do. Jack tried to wiggle loose, but Agatha would not release him. She looked at him carefully and then pulled him in close to her and with their faces so close together Agatha spit the green and red ooze right into Jack's face.

The screams that came from that poor man were deafening. She released him once her vomiting part was over, and he did everything he could to remove the ooze but eventually he fell to the ground and stopped moving all together.

"You see," came a deep dark heavy combined voice, it was a cross between what could be something unheard of trying to enter or something coming up from below toying with them for fun. Whatever it is, it has Agatha and it's using her voice as and body as well.

Chapter 5

Catherine found a slug on the sidewalk and she stepped on it and the squishing sound made her scream. Dorian who was right at the road ready to cross turned around to see and she began laughing at herself and waved him on. Dorian crossed at the crosswalk and Catherine was not that far behind.

The redhead girl bounced into place near his side faster than lightning.

Dorian got to the building and looked at its surprisingly massive size. He was very impressed, from across the street it looked very small and long, but up close it was huge! Catherine was about to make a comment, but Dorian had figured this for some reason and covered her mouth. He looked at the white paint and the mixture of old steel and thought that it was a good mix and that the building could use another paint job here soon. He looked for the door and after about a minute or two he found it. Hidden away in the center of the building was a white door with a bright silver door knob. If it wasn't for the sun hitting it just right Dorian didn't think he'd have found it.

"I was just about to open the door to greet you sir," said a man with light brown hair, he had a mustache and a short goatee on his chin and he wore black colored framed glasses. He had a crook on his nose and his lips were dry and cracked.

"Are you not getting enough water down here?" Dorian asked the man.

"We are, I'm just always like this, anyway, my name's Paul. Pleased to meet you both," and here Paul stuck out his hand and

Dorian shook it and then he shook Catherine's as well, "Follow me and I'll show you what you came to see sir,"

So, the three of them walked down a dimly-lit beige hallway with pictures hanging on both sides of them. Most were in black and white and a good amount were in color, there were some there that were hand drawn. The hand drawn pictures were portraits of different individuals in tall hats some in Napoleon style covers. They all seemed to be in various uniforms, one was civil war – confederate – another was a Frenchman posing like a conquering hero, the last one was Napoleon. The other pictures that hung on the wall were of various people at this building over the years, single and group shots. 'It was a nice time stamp' Dorian thought.

"The pictures that you're staring at Master were taken here, as I'm sure you can tell, but the paintings were given to us," said the mustache man.

"They're nice to look at, I really enjoy them. Thank you, shall we press on?"

"We shall,"

Catherine tugged on Dorian's pant leg and he stopped which caused her to slam into him.

"Are you okay?"

"Yes, I am Master...I mean Dorian sir,"

Suddenly the mustache man appeared out of nowhere, he stood up near them and waved his hand telling them to come on, and Dorian and Catherine began once again to make their way through the hallway.

They came upon two sets of double doors, both were blue-and-white. They opened the first set and there was a smell that overtook them all, the mustache man turned around and said that was Dragon's blood, freshly cooked Dragon's blood. There were a couple of open doors on either side of them, but they didn't dare venture in. The walls in this hallway were coated in red, blue, green, and pink layers of paint that you could see dripping down the center of the wall.

The second double door set led into a room full of offices which also looked like a maze. The mustache man led them through with various twists and turns introducing them to different people and waving hi to others. Each office looked identical, that routinely placed tan and black cubicle material. Some of the people there broke up the monotony of the monotone race by pinning different arrays and assortments of pictures along the sides and back of the walls all held up by thumbtacks.

Once they finally reached the back of the office rows, they were greeted by a large silver steel door with a combination lock on it. The mustache man turned the dial left to the number 10 right to 45 then left to 99, they all heard a click and the door opened wide.

Steam gushed out of the opening door, and though Catherine saw that it was beautiful site (almost alien in her eyes), to everyone else it was a very hot second or two. Once the door was fully opened the three of them walked inside and the door closed behind them. Dorian and Catherine were greeted to the sight and sounds of the locked away, hidden laboratory that only a few knew about, and only a couple out of that few ever visited.

It was here they discovered different vials of red and green liquid being mixed with purple and blues. Beakers held over flames of a Bunsen burner. Different people of all ages were here doing various jobs. There were old men doing what looked like research on the computers on the far-left hand side of the building, and closer to them on the same side were women sweeping the floor and mixing liquid. There were young men and women sitting in the aisle closest to them, and they were wearing funny looking headgear that had lights on all sides that lit up periodically.

The room itself was long, gray, tall, at least 15 feet high, and covered in goop from different failed and successful experiments. The mustache man introduced them to a man in a tailored suit, brown and black with a little white at the cuffs, he said his name was Michael and he's got the key to their research.

"Shall we press on to see it?" he asked. "Sure," Catherine said, and Dorian nodded.

The three of them left the mustache man there and they followed this new man named Michael. Catherine wasn't sure about him, she wasn't sure why either. Could it be the brown hair on his head that was neatly combed back and gelled into place, or was it the scar that crossed over his left eye, or maybe it was those brown puppy dog eyes that she didn't like? Who knows?

They walked down into a narrow corridor with what looked like laboratories from a James Bond movie lining either side. They turned down the first door on the left and walked down a long set of stairs. Dorian and Catherine were studying the blue and the gray and how they mixed well together on the walls in this room, how everyone but them seemed to have lab coats and ID cards. They spied a watercooler in the back of the room on the left and Dorian watched as a few had gathered around it and were talking and laughing.

He looked right and WHAM! He was nosing to nose with a long and large set of mirrors.

"Michael, what's up with these mirrors?" Dorian asked rubbing his nose.

"I will explain, but let's get closer to the beasts, shall we," he leaned forward and gestured for them to start moving once more and they followed him deeper into the laboratory.

They came into a room that was dark, had a pungent order. It was like the smell of rotting fish mixed with the decay of animals. The sting immediately went to their eyes and Catherine couldn't hold it in and had to turn back, Dorian gave chase checking on her.

She had rounded a corner and was hunched over heaving, Dorian had a hold of her red hair and rubbing her back at the same time. Michael walked over to the two of them and handed them masks and apologized for not pointing them out sooner, but he forgot where they were.

"Well, I haven't thrown-up yet Dorian, I think I'll be ok," Catherine said.

"Good, lets get going, I want to see these creatures,"

"As do I,"

"Follow me then," Michael stated once more and motioned for them to join him.

They put their masks on their faces and they re-entered the building. The sting to the eyes was still there, but with the mask on they could handle it. They walked further inward and came into a room full of large black and silver metal cylindrical containers with a casing covering everything but the front glass. As they walked around to the front, Michael directed them up the steps to the top of the stage, "You get a better view of them all from up there. Mind you these are the ones that we believe are no longer here with us. They have shown no sense of being or survival nothing. I shall explain later and have a colleague of mine stop by and we'll go see the remaining few,"

The room which was already dimly lit, suddenly became darker and purple lighting shown onto the "stage" where Michael stood.

"These three subjects here seemed to have perished around the same time, five days after they contracted whatever virus this is. From what we can tell, the souls eyes turn red first, that's stage 1, followed by a case of mumbling incoherent language or words, stage 2. Stage 3 is when the person begins showing hives and small red spots without anything biting him or her. Stage 4 is a hard red near bone like substance grows from those spots and hives, the larger the spots, the larger the Red Horn, we're not sure what else to call it now. This behind me is the 5th and final stage, either the "thing" fully takes over and you go into a paralysis state or you die permanently and go nowhere,"

There was a silence between the three of them, suddenly a door behind them opened that Dorian nor Catherine knew was there. "Master, great to have you here, if you follow me please,"

"Hold on a second," Dorian said placing one hand into the air, and everyone in the room stopped moving, "you're telling me that there are 5 stages to this virus, and we have no idea what it does or is and how long it lasts for, now I'm to follow this guy here in the bright orange lab coat and glasses into some hidden room locked away in some 'vault'?!"

"Precisely," said the technician, "if you two follow me, or if you, Mr. Director, wish to come as well, I have discovered some interesting things about this adversary of ours,"

Dorian hung his head down low and followed Catherine and Michael into the backroom.

There was a pungent odor about the place and Dorian nor Catherine couldn't believe that they were not able to smell it from the other room where all the bodies were being kept. When they all got in and stood in a line they figured out why.

The diseased were walking around the room like they were in some sort of haze, bumping into things and each other. They were all at different stages of infection and the group, Dorian, Catherine and Michael, felt pity and sorrow for these creatures. Catherine noticed that there was one on a silver table in the far back right corner and another one on the left. Dorian spied a group of body bags lining the tan walls all around them at least 4 layers high.

"How long has this disease been going on for and how many have been infected?" Dorian asked.

The technician looked over at him and scratched his curly brown hair, "You know, I'm not sure. There has been a lot and it has been increasing dramatically over the years. While my Patrona is gone, I have pro tempore taken over the position and have been redesigning her work. After all, I am her protégé, and I am learning quickly that she does not like things done in one way constantly,"

The door to the right opened wide and in walked a beautiful woman. She had dark colored skin, brown eyes that could pierce the night sky, long eyelashes that fluttered every time she blinked (Dorian stared at her like she was moving in slow motion), her nose was short and slightly turned up and her high cheekbones gave her that extra boost of innocent beauty. Her chocolate brown hair was long, down to the center of her back and slightly curled at the ends.

"Mylan, you're back early. It's great to see you though. This is Dorian, Catherine and you know the Director,"

"I do, hello everyone, it's great to meet all of you. I am the Lead Scientist and I am investigating the cause of this Redeye issue. We have here in this room various stages of the disease and even though they are loose, they are behind a glass wall for protection. They are my case study, I'm trying to find the cure," Her voice was soothing and angelic, it was like music to Dorian's ears and he wanted to leap out and wrap his arms around her and never let go.

Dorian took a closer look around the room and asked about the body bags and Catherine asked about the tan coloring and why it's not livelier.

"These poor beings...," she began and bowed her head, "they have been through so much. This change that they're going through is hard on them and their loved ones. It's hard enough making the loved ones forget that they were there, but the fact that it seems like they too forget...," she paused once more, "furthermore, the body bags are for those subjects that have completely died, mainly by the hand of one of us,"

"What do you mean? How many have there been?" Dorian asked a little upset and concerned.

"There have been about 1500 known cases. We have kept it all under wraps and plan on keeping it that way. We take great strides in doing so," She looked at Dorian and Catherine carefully and with great concern.

"What is the main story that you tell the families of the victims?" Catherine asked, and Dorian nodded.

"We tell them that their family member has gone on to a better place if their middle aged, if their old we'd say they've moved on to the next plain and if they're young, depending on age, we tell them they went out for a walk and will never return,"

The sound of an alarm bell went off and it got everyone's attention.

The buzzing sound kept blazing loudly and Mylan forced Dorian and Catherine and Michael into a room and slammed the door behind her. They were all breathing heavily waiting to see what was going to happen. The flash of a shadow overtook them for a moment and they all froze, they then saw the eyes of an infected being looking directly at them but not seeing them at all. His eyes were a deep crimson and white in the center and seemed to glow with a demonic type glow. Dorian and Catherine shuffled back as far as they could, but Michael stood in their way and he stopped them from slamming into the wall and making a loud noise.

"How'd they get out? What is going on?" Dorian asked Mylan in a whisper.

"I'm not sure," she replied in the same hushed tone.

The being left the window and Mylan peered out trying to see if there was an opening to which they could escape from. A scream came out from the distance and Catherine jerked a little and clung to Dorian's arm.

There was the sudden sound of a pistol being loaded and a round being placed into the chamber. They all turned their heads and looked at Michael.

"You know as well as I do that that's not going to work. We're already dead to begin with," Mylan stated to him.

"I know, but I still want to try," Michael replied.

Michael stepped closer to the door, "Mylan, open the door for me and I'll find us an escape route. If I get into any danger I have this to try to defend myself with," He held up his pistol and Mylan reluctantly nodded her head.

She opened wide the door and as soon as he was out, it was closed once more and the three of them were taking turns looking out the small rectangular piece of glass.

Dorian saw three of the diseased walking in the far back corner by the other door where he noticed Michael was. He notified the girls of what was going on and they tried to get inch their way under and beside him so that they too had a view. With Dorian being 6 feet 7 inches, it was hard enough hunching over to look out this window for an extended period (without kneeling) but he did, he stood as far back as he could and as high up on the window as possible. Catherine came in underneath and she squatted low where it was just her eyes and the top of her red hair showing, Mylan stood in the center and they all watched Michael.

Dorian whispered that he was hiding in the debris in the back, near the two-tall green and black garbage cans. They saw the door in the back- burst wide open and screaming inward was a blonde woman in a white lab coat with pins and stickers all over it.

"I don't want to die! Somebody help me!"

Then came the fourth infected and it grabbed a hold of her and brought her to the ground. Dorian, Catherine and Mylan watched carefully from their hideaway and Michael watched from his. A few moments later she rose to her feet and brushed herself off and looked around the room.

"I'm fine, I'm still alive! I better get home to my kids, I can't take this anymore," She said and walked to another door just out of sight and opened it wide and walked out leaving the door wide open. The infected followed her not long after.

Michael got out from his spot and went over to Dorian's door and opened it wide and said that the creatures were gone and were now running the country side.

"We need to stop this disease, and them before it takes over Nebula and destroys everything," Mylan stated and the rest nodded.

"What can we do?" Dorian asked.

"We need someone who can get infected and allow me to study them for a cure,"

"Could there be another way?" Catherine questioned.

"If there is I'd like to know about it. I'm familiar with the science side of things,"

"We'll see what we can do Mylan," Michael stated.

Just as the four of them began to make their plans a sky-blue car pulled up in front the white building and honked its horn 3 times. They didn't move, and the driver of the vehicle got out, he was a burly man, he wore a black shirt with white writing on it but none of them could read it, they noticed he had a moustache and a beard and they were both red in color, as well as the hair on his head.

He walked up to them and pointed and said, "You 4, come. Master is waiting. Best not keep her waiting or else," His voice grumbled in a deep, dark and yet a little scratchy, kind of like he had been coughing a few minutes prior to pulling up. He needed some water Mylan was sure of.

"Or else what?" Michael asked.

"She will release more sub servants out into this plain of existence,"

"Why?" Dorian asked him.

"Last time, she took over a planet,"

The 4 of them looked at each other and they all got into the sky-blue vehicle. The driver followed right behind them and he started the car and drove off to 401 Dragon Den Boulevard.

Chapter 6

Veronica and Jack stood there watching Agatha as she seemed to transform into this new being. The other gentleman that was with them was caught in her grasp.

"Please release me Agatha,"

"We are not Agatha anymore," the triple voice said. It was so dark and frightening that Veronica shivered and began to tear up.

Jack stood tall and asked her, "Who did you send for?"

"I sent for the 2 that have been in my way and the 2 that have gone to become in my way,"

"What are you? Who are you?" Veronica asked Agatha.

"Who are you to demand answers from me puny being?" Agatha said. Veronica looked at her and if looks could kill, Agatha would have fallen over on the spot. Jack walked up beside Veronica and grabbed her and walked her back a few steps.

A sky-blue car pulled up and parked out front of the destructed building and five people got out. Veronica saw Dorian and she immediately took off towards him on a dead run and slammed right into Agatha's open arm.

"What in the world? Agatha, how'd you get over here so fast?" Jack and Veronica asked.

"We see that he has a lover, now girl, hold your tongue and position," Agatha stated.

Dorian reached his hand inside the car and helped a Catherine and Michael and Mylan were on the other side getting out as well. Dorian's eyes were in utter disbelief when he looked upon the destruction of the building. He noticed that the whole place was destroyed and some of the surrounding area as well. There was a small fire burning where the kitchen once was and another one where his room was as well. Dorian heard sobs coming from his left and he looked down and he noticed Catherine was crying.

Dorian looked all over for survivors and began to walk towards the destructed property. The bearded man grabbed hold of Dorian's shoulder and shook his head and pointed to the right of the building. There Dorian saw 4 people standing, Agatha, Jack, Veronica and someone in a Hawaiian shirt.

The bearded man led them over to the other group and Veronica heart wanted to leap out of her body and jump into Dorian's and burry itself in his.

Once both groups collided the sun set and darkness over took the world.

NIGHT 1:

"Now that we are here, I want to thank all of you for being such gracious hosts. Except for you. You can leave," Agatha said with her multiple voices at the same time while pointing at the man in the Hawaiian shirt. He looked at her cautiously and took off as fast as he possibly could.

Dorian stared at Agatha with a new set of eyes. "Agatha, you're different? What's changed in you?"

"Don't you like it Dorian? Am I not the one you love anymore," She boomed.

"Dorian, you loved her?" Catherine asked in a whisper.

"I used her for a ceremony and sacrificed her. It wasn't long after that when I found my way here and met you,"

Catherine said nothing, she just stared at Dorian with eyes that said that she wanted him, and she understood him.

"Ma'am," began the man with the beard who came over and kneeled in front of her, "ma'am, I worship you and your very essence, even though I know that this is not your true form. I humbly ask to join you in your glorious transformation,"

Agatha stared at the burly man who was begging to join her, "We allow you to integrate with us," Agatha reached down, and this athletically built woman easily lifted what looked like a 300 to 400-pound man with one hand. Comparing the two of them, Agatha was a petite woman, and you'd never dream or think she'd ever be able to lift that man by one hand. "You shall now be integrated," She was saying to him while beginning to pull his body into hers.

The six others could not believe what they were seeing, and Jack was trying to figure out a way to get everyone out of there. He called Dorian back and the two of them started talking and Dorian told Jack of Michael's weapon and Michael was called in.

While the boys were having a conversation, the girls were too. Mylan and Veronica compared notes and then they compared those notes to that of what Catherine knew and none of them can figure out what this entity is that has invaded Agatha's body and mind.

They all have come to the same conclusion though…it controls the redeye beings.

"You six," Agatha began pointing at the group, her mixed voices sounding more joined and demonic then before, "you shall bear witness to a new beginning, I shall reorganize this world and none of you can stop it for it has already begun,"

Agatha rose to an even higher standing position, Dorian and Catherine noticed that her feet were no longer on the ground, and she let out a screech that sounded like a mixture of a Banshee and a Sirens call. At the same time Michael and Jack felt a lure to join her and be with her, while Veronica and Mylan had to cover their ears and felt a deeper hatred towards her.

Dorian stepped forward along with Catherine and reached out for Agatha, she slapped their hands away and screamed into their faces.

"Agatha! Please come back to us!" Dorian screamed back at her.

"It's no longer just Agatha, Dorian," She said saying Dorian's name a little sharply.

Agatha raised her hand, and as it began to fall Catherine shoved Dorian out of harm's way and took a shockingly hard to her face. It rocked Catherine back and nearly sent her flying, but the redhead came back strong and with a couple punches of her own she sent Agatha running into the corner. Agatha was stunned, she couldn't believe that this scrawny little redhead girl could hit the way she does, but the next thing Agatha knew, another blow to the face rocked her world upside down.

Agatha rose to her feet clutching a round piece of rusted metal. She banged it against some of the others that looked just like it and shook off a good amount of it and charged after Catherine with it. Catherine ducked and rolled under the swinging object and slid one the grass a couple feet and inadvertently found one herself. She lifted it and brushed it off.

"Fair game again, huh,"

Agatha screeched, and the moon got covered up by cloud and both stopped for a moment. Agatha, mainly thinking she did that herself and Catherine because it's hard to see without the moon light.

Once the light returned the ladies were back at it again. The rebar clanging together making its dulling noisy sound.

"Why do you fight for him? He doesn't love you," Agatha said.

"You…Don't …know…that!" Catherine said fighting her off and finally pinning her rebar sword to the ground, "Is that what this is all about?!"

Agatha placed her hands on her head and began screaming like a banshee, everyone dropped to the ground and covered their ears and closed their eyes. They all heard her thoughts: 'This is not the last, middle nor the end. This is only the first, the beginning, beware for if you challenge me again I may not be so nice.'

"She seems to be gone," Dorian said rising to his feet.

"Ouch – are you sure she's gone – ouch?!" Veronica questioned as she was rising off the ground.

"Are you okay Mylan? What about you Jack? Michael?" Dorian had called out looking around for everybody. Each one of them sounded off and then he turned and called for Catherine, who he found up near the top of the road.

"You know Dorian, I had her. And just a few more seconds she would never have escaped and then maybe, just maybe, you'd gotten your friend back,"

Dorian wrapped his arms around Catherine tightly and whispered into her ear that he's happy that he has her and he wouldn't trade her for anything in the world.

The other members of the group made their way to the top of the road where Dorian and Catherine stood, the all turned and faced the new demolished building, then they turned right (as per Catherine suggestion) and began walking towards an unknown destination.

"I have a friend that lives right down the road from here, she'll give us a place to stay for the night. And for good, maybe a little bit longer," Catherine stated.

"Let's hope your friend doesn't mind this many people," Veronica said, Jack and Michael nodded, and Mylan just shrugged her shoulders.

Dorian kept a straight face and just walk forward, it was like he didn't care.

They walked slowly, cautiously, and massively on edge. Any sound that came out made them jump and huddle close together. They kind of figured that the redeye beings lurking everywhere.

"How much further?' came the whispers from the back. "Not much more, we're almost there,"

They carefully walked through a couple of neighborhoods, checking around every corner, double checking every vacant lot, they weren't sure what would become of them if they were touched by one of those redeye beings. They did not want to find out either. Still they pressed on with Catherine leading the way, she led them into one neighborhood where under the moonlight everything looked a pale shade of blue.

Here there's a mixture of houses and double wide trailers, and a lot of their windows if not all of them seem to be facing up towards the road. And in each window, it was either a candle or some sort of light gave an eerie glow to the yard or to the nearby area around it. The first house on the left, as they approached it, appeared to have a long porch, tall with pillars at the front of the porch holding it up, and led up to pale front door with two windows on the left and right side of it. In both of those windows they were to menorah candles and each set casts its ghost along porch floor.

The trailer diagonal from it had wooden stairs going up to the door, on the edges of the wooden steps were battery-operated candles, on a pathway from the driveway to the to the stairs there were solar lights. The trailer must've been white because under the moonlight it had a very bluish tint to it. The window facing the road had a plain white flag behind a green light, and its window curtains were black as if to emphasize the light even more.

They looked at houses like this very similar as a kept walking down the street. They came upon Ion Street and Catherine turned right there and let them down three houses and turn left and walked on to a house that was full of life.

The whole property was lit up, for the top of the driveway to the porch, the group even figured the backyard was lit up as well. They heard music playing laughter and a lot of loud talking and music. The house was golden brown and had a black trim. It was a two-story house and from what could be seen from the road there were steps on the left-hand side going up, coming from those steps there was up a sidewalk leading towards the driveway with lights on both sides to guide your way. They could see the Windows on the second floor and noticed the people all dancing and talking nearby the window. They notice there are two more windows up at the top, but I couldn't quite tell what they were because they were blocked by roof of another window. Michael noted that there was a lot of plant life and greenery on the grounds, he brought that attention to Mylan. The door opened wide and then Catherine made a motion waving everyone on and they all followed her inward.

The house had a very long porch, rocking chair on the left, a swing on the right and then center was the door. Just to the right of the door there were two chairs and a table in the center of them, there was an ashtray on that table with no sign of any cigarette ever being placed there.

"Come on in, everyone is welcome," said the tall man's the door. "Is Michelle here?" Catherine asked.

"Not at the moment, but you're welcome to stay until she gets back," said the tall man they stood to the side on the door wide open and the group walked inside with Catherine leading the way. As Dorian passed by the man, he noticed the he was dressed in all-black and on his shirt, there was a red A in a circle, seem to be the only color on him. He also observed that they were chains coming from his waist to his pocket, a chain around his neck in the shape of little silver balls, Dorian thought that this person might be wearing makeup, but he was not 100% sure.

The place was packed there was barely enough room for them and as the door closed behind them they just huddled close together.

"Calm down, join us. It's our end of the world party," said the tall man.

"End of the world party? What you mean?" Mylan questioned.

"Like, the new age goddess shall rise from her ashes, torment the LIVING, and burn the world to ash, and like, making it possible for us to join her in the New World!" Said some blonde headed woman dressed very similar to the tall man standing in front of them.

"Is Michelle into this now?" Catherine asked.

"Yes, she is our leader," said the tall man.

Just at that moment the back door opened wide and walked another redhead woman carrying an armful of groceries. She held similar attire to the tall man and to the blonde headed woman, plaid colored miniskirt and knee-high boots, stockings, a belly button ring with the same red circled A symbol, in both ears she had three rows of piercings, in both eyebrows there was also a piercing. Her hair was long and looked very knotted up, and she had a very pale complexion. Much like anyone at this party that they've noticed so far accept this person seem to have a more advanced paleness. She had a monopoly on the black department though, she was covered in it. The only other color she had on her face was her ruby red lips.

"I'm coming Michelle!" Catherine hollered as she ran towards this person.

Suddenly the glass shattered and screams echo through the house!

Chapter 7

Under the pressures of the entity being inside of her, Agatha does all she can to keep herself as sane as possible. It's becoming taxing on her especially because your thoughts are no longer becoming her own, they're being merged with the beings that's inside of her. She often wonders how long she can hold out. She has tried numerous times to break free of this being, but its grasp of hers is too strong and for some reason it refuses to let go of her. She can somewhat see what is happening, but sadly she has no control over her own body anymore she can't stop what's going on.

It's an interesting feat that has been accomplished here, she is taking her soul into someone else's – rather someone else has invaded her soul, and since Agatha is pure spirit anyway she had to naturally figure out a way to make room for those of the entity to come in. How this is done, it, like a magician's box. The box has three sides and the lid, the assistant crawls inside the box in magician shows that consisted still there he lays a blanket or cloth on top of the box and covers the box completely, says his or her magic words and proof the assistant has vanished without a trace. They lifted the opening to a hole in the bottom and stayed there until the coast was clear and slipped out the box. If a magician called for them to reappear, they stayed in the box, which is more than likely the case.

With the above example that is what's going on with Agatha. Since she is a natural channeller for the LIVING, she does this naturally without even knowing it. Somehow this being took notice of Agatha and now has taken full advantage of her.

"How long you keep me prisoner here?" Agatha asked the being.

"As long as necessary. I can't be here without you, so until my task is complete I shall remain a part of you as a permanent fixture," the being said in its and its triple sounding voice. She was rather upset because one of those voices was her own, but it was using, and she was powerless to stop it.

"What do I call you? I don't know your name,"

"I am Zero, you are Agatha. There, we've met. Is there anything else?" Zero said annoyed and its triple voice.

"What are you after Zero?" Agatha asked as innocently as possible.

"I am after my family. You see Agatha, they were taken from me long ago by a Beast. Murdered in front of my eyes. I am here to see them. I hope they are here,"

"If you would have said something like that in the first place instead of destroyed and harmed, or worse, like you have, than we could've done something freely then. You don't need to hold me hostage,"

Agatha/Zero walked towards Plummet Street and a whole army of redeye beings followed close behind her/them.

"Zero," Agatha started and then paused for a moment, "the Army that's following behind us makes me a little uneasy."

"Get used to it Agatha. There may be more joining us soon."

Agatha could barely see out of her own eyes, and her thoughts were barely her own. To Agatha felt like this was no longer a merger, but a complete takeover and she was not sure how much longer she could hold out before Zero would took over.

The street alone was barely lit, just a few streetlights that flickered on and off as they walked by. Agatha/Zero continued onward. Every third house, two or three of the redeye creatures would dissent from among the ranks and rummaged through the house looking for lost souls to join their ranks. Agatha was shocked by the fact there was no cars on the road, no one walking, not a soul to be found. It was like they all knew something was of danger, but they couldn't quite place it. Suddenly and quite unexpectedly out of her body stopped moving on its own.

"I hear them." Zero said in her triple voice.

Agatha's head turned right, and Agatha barely caught a glimpse of a bluish looking trailer and a man that looked like Dorian sitting on a rocking chair. The man rose to his feet and knocked on the glass window three times and a whole horde of people came flooding onto the driveway. Many of them started bowing and praying at Agatha's feet while six of them stood strong and poised to attack.

"So, this is where you weaklings decided to go to. I must admit, I expected a lot more from you." Agatha said with her triple voice.

"Agatha, please come back to us," Dorian began pleading to her, "we don't want to harm you."

Agatha/Zero fully turned facing them and raised her right hand and a light began to shine from it. A smile came across her face and Agatha was appalled by it, yet she felt like she had no control of herself anymore. Her right arm twirled around in big circles and suddenly she plunged it inward and the light buried deep into Agatha's chest and they flew back into the brick building behind them.

As the dust began to clear the six of them noticed that Agatha was on the ground and a new figure was standing before them. She was medium height and had light brown hair, she took on more of Agatha's appearance than her own but there was something more to this being than just looks. The being walked towards the six of them that wee still standing and smiled. With a wave of her hand the people that wee their sill kneeling and bowing to her began to change and take on a form that all too familiar to Mylan and Michael.

"Run!" They both shouted. "What about Agatha?"

"Forget about her! We gotta save ourselves! Move Dorian!"

Dorian watched as the new figure bent over and picked up Agatha by the hair and disappeared into the darkness and then he glanced behind him and he hollered out to the group to pick up the pace. The redeye creatures were closing in fast and it appeared that they were not letting up anytime soon. The creatures split up into two groups, one took a street to the right and the others stayed on the groups heels.

The darkness before them began to clear as the streetlights stared to turn back on one after another. Catherine, who was running the fastest took a sharp right leading the group towards a bunker where they maybe able to hide for the rest of the night and formulate some sort of plan, when as soon as it was in sight a small group of redeyes appeared from it leaping from behind and overtop, charging at them from the front with the group of redeyes still nipping at their heels.

Agatha was tightly bound while standing on some sort of stone block. Her head was all hazy from the light that had entered her, and she felt like she was going to be sick. She started moving but despite her attempts, she was unable to and unable to loosen the ropes that held her prisoner. She looked around as best she could and noticed some things that looked a little familiar and things that did not. She was not too sure where she was nor, did she know what was going to happen to her.

"Ah, you're awake. So now we can begin." Said an unfamiliar voice.

"Who are you? Where are you?" Agatha cried out.

"I am here. I come from within Agatha." It spoke once more, this time with a more menacingly tone.

Agatha's body quivered, and she did not like the sudden feeling that she had. She felt like she was going to die permanently from whatever this voice was. She glanced around the room as best she could looking for something, someone, but with her eyesight the way that it was she could barely see 5 feet in front of her. Suddenly (unless her eyes were playing tricks on her), she noticed a shadow dart from left to right and then right to left and then left to right once more.

Agatha begun to scream, she was surprised at how much volume she did get out of her little body, but she felt it wasn't enough to alarm anyone. She did hope someone was nearby. The figure that darted left and right stood from the shadows and walked to Agatha's point of view. Agatha was amazed it was a young woman that looked nearly identical to her.

"Zero?"

"Yes Agatha."

"What have you done? Why do you look like me?" Agatha questioned as best she could.

"I needed to host. And now that I have you, I can keep you locked away and no one will find you." The smile on Zero's space widened. She began rubbing her hands together and twisting them in all sorts of different manners it looked rather unhuman. Zero walked up to Agatha and pulled out a knife, she waved it in front of Agatha's face and smiled.

"Zero, what are you going to do with that?" Agatha asked terrified.

Zero rubbed the back end of the knife across Agatha's cheek with the curved end barely cutting into her skin. She then pulled it away closing the knife and moved to the other side of Agatha's body where she began licking the blood that was dripping down.

Agatha pulled up the ropes with every lick as hard as she could. Zero only smiled at her. With zero is finished licking Agatha's wound, she kissed her cheek and told Agatha not to worry that she'd be freed soon.

Mylan, Dorian, Catherine, Veronica, Michael and Jack decide to split the multiple parties and dispersed throughout the city. They had decided on a meeting point, the fountain in the center of the city. Dorian had suggested that they meet there in an hour, but Jack said that that all meet there as soon as they could get rid of the redeye creatures that were following them.

Dorian and Catherine had made it to a bunker and they were hiding out inside of it waiting for the redeye creatures to pass by. Mylan and Michael were running on top of the rooftops of different building heading towards the fountain one step ahead of the redeye creatures that were below them. Veronica and Jack were stuck in an alleyway surrounded by the redeye creatures. The creatures weren't attacking them they just stood there whispering towards them. Veronica was screaming at them Jack was trying to calm Veronica down, but it was doing no good. Veronica picked up a piece of wood from the ground and held it in her hand like it was some sort of sword and was ready to attack the redeye creatures as soon as they took one step towards her.

One redeye creature to the left of Veronica began stumbling towards her with his arms stretched out. Veronica screamed loudly and swung wildly cold clocking the creature in the back of its head, and when the creature fell to the ground the rest of them began charging in.

Dorian and Catherine heard her scream and watched as the redeye creatures that were in front of them turned away and ran towards it. They looked at one another and fear came over top of them, they both bolted out from the bunker running towards the sound of Veronica's screams.

Mylan and Michael had arrived at the fountain and by the time they got there they had noticed that their followers were no longer following them. They had no idea when they lost them but all aid they knew was that they weren't being followed anymore. They heard a faint echo of the scream, but they weren't sure where it came from. As they looked around the area they notice that nothing was touched, no creatures were there, and everything seemed to be normal.

As Dorian and Catherine around the corner they had to stop in their tracks immediately. They notice a whole horde of redeye creatures standing there. The Army was so massive that Dorian didn't dare bother counting.

Dorian did notice that the creatures did not know how to climb, and he pointed this out to Catherine. So, the two of them looked up towards the tops of the buildings and noticed that there was a stairwell that led to the rooftop and so they took it. Leaping from one building to the next thing a perfect view of the site and the redeye creatures were looking at.

Jack was laying on the ground and he was convulsing. The redeye creatures were on top of him pulling him back towards their crowd and Veronica was swinging her stick wildly at them screaming her head off.

Dorian looked at Catherine and whispered to her: "Michael would be nice right now after all he's got the gun."

Dorian and Catherine look to the right and they watched as the creatures began to part way for a mysterious hooded figure who began walking through the crowd. It was like this figure was floating on air as it walked. As it passed through the crowd the figure touched the head of the creatures to the right into the left. Those creatures began to morph into something else, something scarier, something more powerful.

The creatures began to grow and shake violently. They look like abominable snowman with sharp ragged pointing glass shards coming out of their skin. The glass was red their arms were red, their legs were red, but their torsos and heads were the color of their natural skin. Suddenly there came a monstrous cry, then another and another, soon the night echoed with their monstrous cries and all of them had turned and faced the building where Dorian and Catherine were laying and looking onward.

Dorian rose to his feet grabbing Catherine within his hand, "That's our queue," Dorian hollered out and he with Catherine's hand in his rushed towards the next building and down the fire escape, heading back towards the bunker. They ran as fast as they could, Dorian nearly pulling Catherine along with him. Catherine's body jerked every so often though she wanted to complain she never did.

It was after a couple blocks Dorian looked over his shoulder and noticed that the creatures were not following him, so he slowed his pace. Catherine had to stop and catch her breath she placed her hands on her knees and was nearly bent all the way over. That's when they heard the sounds, the scratching of the feet across the hard service, the distant mumbling. Catherine stood straight up and looked over her left shoulder and Dorian looked directly over hers and together they notice the creatures were beginning to show their faces.

"Forgot in some, forgotten son, rape of Eve," these creatures were muttering the same as they rounded the corner.

"Dorian... Dorian... You can't hide from me. We will find you." Came a call from above. Dorian looked up and saw hooded figure floating above the street he was standing on. It looked down on him and Dorian could've sworn that he saw a faint smile come across the figures face. "Dorian, I have a present for you. I think you'll quite like her now, I find her more enjoyable." In the hooded figures finger pointed to the front row and Dorian had to take a step back because there was Veronica blonde hair flowing, and her purple and black striped dress, with red glass shards coming out of her skin.

"I'm going to stop you. Where is Agatha? What have you done to her?" Dorian demanded.

"She's here." And the figure turned and turned its back and Dorian heard couple straps come loose, and he watches Agatha dropped from the sky. He ran underneath of her as quickly as he could to catch her, but he missed, and instead she bounced off the pavement and right into his arms. She was ice cold it his touch and he shook her a few times, but she did not wake so he pulled her tightly into his body and he and Catherine began running for their lives once more.

They rounded the corner from Rose Street to Plymouth where they spied a World War II bunker sitting in the far back right in corner and the three of them found their way inside the bunker locked the door and clung there for the night.

Chapter 8

Day 2:

Mylan and Michael woke to the sounds of happiness and joyfulness, loud music people cheering and all sorts of excitement happening all around them. Michael looked over at Mylan with a puzzled look on his face. He noticed that Mylan had a puzzled look on hers as well. They both noticed that there were doodles and all sorts of fun drawings all over their faces as well and they both laughed at each other's expenses.

They both took a quick look around and noticed that there are all sorts of people outside were wandering around and that everyone looked normal like there was nothing wrong with them and that there was nothing to worry about, like nothing happened by the night before. They both rose off the fountain and walked over to a young woman in a red and black shirt and asked her about the night before, to their dismay she knew nothing about it and said that it was a normal quiet night with her and her family.

So, they asked about 10 other people and the same response came across the same 10 people's faces, puzzlement and then they got the same response. So, they looked at each other and they wondered if the if the just imagined the events from the night before.

Mylan and Michael decided to make the most of this exciting moment, and they decided to get on a couple of the amusement rides that were in the middle of the area. They first got on the Riptide roller coaster ride, and then they got on the Spinning Teacups. Michael made a feat at the "Show your Strength", Mylan clinging to Michael's arm for the rest of the day as they tried out different games and rides.

The afternoon sun was just starting to fade when she arrived.

Veronica looked radiant as ever, her long flowing blonde hair not tangling in the breeze, just steadily flowing behind her. She was in a red top with black pants and she was waving hi to them as she was running up, when she got to Mylan and Michael she was nothing but smiles.

"So, are you guys ready for tonight?"

"Yes, Veronica we are." Mylan said.

Dorian, Catherine and Agatha were hiding out in a bunker when the light began to touch their faces. At first Catherine complained but then she rolled over to Dorian's arms and everything was okay. Dorian had Agatha in his other arm and they were leaning up against the back wall ever so tightly.

Suddenly there was some loud banging on the door and Dorian and the girls awoke with a start! The claw marks scratching at the door and the grinding of glass in the metal made this squeal that pierced their ears. Dorian quickly realized that they had nowhere to go and he looked on the ground for some sort of weapon to fight them back off with.

There was nothing to be found, and Dorian stood in front of the girls as the door burst wide open. The creatures stumbled inside, and they stood within a few feet of Dorian and stopped and just stared at them. They were all muttering something, but no one can make out what they were saying.

Suddenly they all stood sideways, and a hooded figure came walking in word with a devious smile on her face.

"You are the last three. Come with me or die."

Dorian, Catherine and Agatha nodded. Even though they knew this figure was, they did not want to take their chances in a small confined space where they had nowhere to go.

"I have something I want to tell you." Zero said. "What's that?" Agatha asked.

"I have found my family."

"So, this whole business can be done with, right?" Dorian stated with a harsher tone.

"Not quite yet. I want to find out why I can't die."

Agatha reached out and touched Zero's left shoulder. And it was like time had stopped for Agatha in Zero. Suddenly Agatha was transferred, and all her thoughts and mind were in the past. This is what she saw thought and heard:

"I come from the land in the distant past, where the Earth was relatively new to mankind and farming was still predominantly done by hand. I was in a small village, there were horses, cows, oxen, plenty of birds of all variety. There were a small number of children. Most of the time the women died giving birth, and those that did survive childbirth most of their children died during the early years of their lives.

"But we were a small village and we took care of our own as best we could. We farmed the fields every day, the hunters hunted daily, and the women were sewing and mending and did various other jobs. Money really didn't exist. We had a barter system, worked on trade mostly.

"It was mostly wood structures that line the streets. The butcher (I guess that's what you would call him, that's what they referred them now as) had a little hut on the left of the fire circle, he hung meat there from the sides of his awning. He was a tall man, very chunky, he had long dark hair, he had squared chin with a cleft in the middle and beautiful deep blue eyes, the likes of which I've never seen again. He had the most remarkable nose I've ever seen on a human being before, it was long, rounded at the end but it didn't flare out, it was small and short very narrow. He did have a bulging forehead though, it wasn't that bad, but it did stick out a bit.

"Our leader, our Chief, whatever you want to call him, was the greatest person in the entire world, even better than my Dad. While my Dad went out hunting all day, came home ate my Mom's cooking and then slept, the Chief took care of business all day. From dealing with people just walking up to him asking him questions and complaining about different things, to asking different people take care of different things for him to try to make the village a better place. Unlike the butcher whose clothes were stained with blood, the Chief's clothes were set apart unlike anyone else's, they were the talk of the village.

There were times where he wore brown jackets with a white undershirt or black jackets with an off-white undershirt, but always in black pants. When his wife passed away he never took the time to learn how to make clothing and he wasn't paid enough to buy some off the seamstress in town, so he would ask one of the local maidens to make his clothing. Many did it for free, others charged very little or for an extra scrap of food.

"The seamstress was a bitter old maid that no one really liked but how everyone loved her work. Her small hut was on the opposite side of the butchers on the fire circle. On the ground surrounding her were her goods, clothing, blankets, and other belongings, some hers and some other people (like her granddaughter) made. She took meat, grain, and fabric as well as old clothing that can be reused as goods towards the purchase of her items. Her prices were steep, but the trade credit was usually just as high. It was good.

"The people were dressed in mainly browns and blacks. There were some white shirts thrown in there but most of the time with the kind of work that was done the white shirts were either saved for important events (celebrations or funerals) or they became brown from all the dirt and dust. It was very bland.

"While I was in the seamstress's hut I heard a loud commotion coming from the woods. The other men in the village began running towards it and hollered back to us to fetch water from the well. I dropped the dress I was looking at on the ground and ran out towards the commotion.

"The woods weren't very far from the village, they were practically on top of it."

The woods surrounded the village on three sides and a river was on the fourth. The woods were full of tall pine, maple and sycamore trees, and plenty of game in between. The hunters would go out into the woods and hunt for various types of animals, and they usually succeeded in finding enough for all of us. At the same time, there were also the gatherers, they'd go out with the hunters and pick the berries and plants and other objects that we needed to go with our food, clothing, makeup or medicine. I wanted to be a hunter, but a girl is not a hunter.

"I ran towards the commotion, dropping the dress on the ground and as soon as I rounded the corner, the sight hit me like a ton of bricks! My father's arms were shredded and dangling, the skin on his arms was folded outward and jagged lines are all that remain. You could see his arm muscles, both, the red gooey, lined substance that you cannot imagine, that's what everyone saw. That wasn't the worst of it, as I was looking my Dad over, I realized that his legs were gone too! I couldn't believe it! What could do this to him?

"Then a Beast roared in the distance and there was more screaming, then another roar, this one was closer. This continued like this for a while until the Beast was right on our door step. I hate to say it, but with the way that this Beast was, my Dad was put on hold, he was bandaged as best as possible, but not cared for like the Chief would have been.

"The Beast breathed down our necks, I don't know about everyone else, but I could feel it as it entered the village. This dreadful feeling, full of pain and suffering the like of which we've never known before. The Beast entered from the South gate, I was at the East gate, there were guards at the North as well at the West. I heard its ferocious roar as it entered our village, the screams and cries from the villagers as either they were killed or ran away, and the Beast's fierce screams sent shockwaves through my ears.

"My curiosity was on high, my thoughts seemed to be not my own, but for a moment, I wanted to see it, to see the Beast that is killing my village people. That's when it came forward, it wasn't all at once like some lumbering behemoth, but it came at us in fast fluid motions like it had the speed of man and wolf mixed together.

"The Beast was tall like a brown bear, black with white spotted fur covering its body, it had no horns on its head, but it did have sharpened claws on all 4 of its paws, which the Beast used quite well.

I watched helplessly as a small girl no older than my youngest sister get sliced and shredded by this horrible monster. I bore witness to the savage killing of my people, and I didn't know why. Its snout was long and squared, its nose was a dark black – blacker than night – its teeth were dripping with the blood of the people that it just killed.

"The Beast approached the fire circle, it raised its snout in the air like it was following the scent of something. I wasn't sure what, I looked at the different things it could be, the butchers – with all his meat hanging out, or was it the fire itself? Could it be the fact of the burning of the young animal the other night by us (the whole village) sent this Beast off the way it is? But we needed the food, and so did the gods? Why were we to be punished for that? We've always done that?

"The Beast approached a meat stick and ate for a few minutes, during this time many of our men tried to subdue this horrendous creature and destroy it, but it was to no avail. We all wondered why the Beast was eating, did it not get it's fill from killing our people? Instead, the Beast just flicked a piece of bone right into one heart after the next until they stopped and let it eat in peace. It demolished all the butcher's supply, but the butcher didn't care, the Beast had him pinned to the ground between its back-right paw, right at the second or third sharp claw. No man dared to venture in to try to rescue him, the butcher…was on his own.

"I turned towards my Dad who was lying on the ground gasping for air. I rushed over to him and grabbed a hold of his head. I told him that I loved him and that I was there for him. He replied to me with a smile, the best one he could muster.

"There I sat, with my Dad's head on my lap and he was taking his last. I'm happy one of us was able to be here (accident or not). At least he wasn't alone. I said to my Dad, 'Dad, I know…how hard it is for you right now…' I sniffled here, and tears fell from my face, 'but you have to let go…' the tears fell hard on top of his face and all over the ground beside us, 'I understand, and I'll take care of Mom and Anita, you need to take care of you. Go Dad, let the Spirits of Old Take you on your Journey.' The light faded from my father's eyes and he died on my lap. I closed his eyes for him and gently placed his head on the ground and prayed that he's be safe.

"The seamstress returned to her hut screaming and crying, when she looked at my father she burst out and even more tears. I had no idea she felt this way about anyone, she always seems so cold and cruel. The redness in her eyes and her cheeks told me that these tears were for real and they match my own, and led me to ask the question: who did you lose? The seamstress replied one word, between her muffled cheers and screams I only understood the one word... Granddaughter. Then out of the blue the Beast began to move again the villagers started screaming and hollering, all trying to stab the Beast various items knives, spears, whatever they could find, but nothing seemed to be working. Nothing would penetrate the Beast skin.

"That's when it happened, this is the time when I went berserk. I heard my mother scream a terrifying scream, a scream of life and death, a scream of pain and suffering and agony and everything in between all rolled into one. It was such a terrifying scream that the Beast even curled away in fear. I ran out of the seamstress's hut and got where can see the carnage by the butcher's hut, there I spied my Mom and my sister Anita. Anita was standing in the way the Beast, she was holding it flowers up to it thinking that maybe something sweet with soothe the Beast, but my poor sister could not have been more wrong.

"I watched my mother scream again and charged the Beast headlong, I began to run down towards her thinking that if my Mom could get to the Beast, I could save Anita. As I ran I watched the men start poking it with spears and sticks as my Mom jumped on the Beast's back, a man handed her a stick, or a spear and she jabbed it in between his shoulder blades and neck. I wash the blood flew out and she was covered in it, the Beast roared a terrible terrifying cry and then it shook her off and just as soon as I got down there the Beast pinned her down and bit off her head.

"Terror, pain, anger, rage, every emotion imaginable rushed through my veins all at once. I felt unstoppable, like I was a GOD.

I just lost my father, he died in my lap, now the Beast just ripped off my mother's head… The Beast is mine.

"I was in full sprint mode, no being alive could catch me. It was a race against time and the Beast…claws versus Anita. I ran fast and hard, her dirty-blonde hair was blowing in the wind, I knew she was looking up at death's face…

"By the time I got to her, I watched as the Beast sliced her in half, it was like one stroke for it. One single stroke and the Beast took out the entire life time of memories, joy, sadness, love and everything in between. The Beast has been doing this for some time now, I turned and glared right into the Beast's face. I was not frightened, nor was I scared. I was terrified. I gathered up all my courage, I grabbed two spears from the men beside me and charged at the Beast.

"The Beast roared, this roar would terrify any living man or woman, but I didn't care, it took my family, it took my friends, the damn thing had to die!

"It didn't take me long to reach the Beast, and as soon as I did I plunged 1 spear right into its eyes and stepped on its snout and ran up to the other spear that my mother inserted in the Beast neck and put my second spear right beside hers. I wiggled both spears back and forth like a cutting motion. The Beast bucked and screamed and cried, and then rolled pinning me to the ground, and then got from me and with its mighty paw the Beast pressed all its weight down on my legs, then took its claw which was as long as my legs and sliced open my chest. I felt everything.

"It then pulled me in close, I thought I was dead, but it didn't kill me. It dropped three tears into my open chest, then like magic my chest sealed itself and the Beast fell over at that point it did not move again.

"As time went on I noticed as well as the villagers that I never aged, and they did. They also noticed that I developed quite well, it took a while, but I did. And every man in the village wanted me but were told to stay away from me because there was something not right about me.

"I watched the village rise to power and become an Empire, I did all that from a distance, mainly because I was not allowed in the village anymore. I learned how to hunt and fish and gather supplies on my own, I also learned from the local outcasts different forms of magic per se (lack of wording, not sure what else to call it).

"It is from these people that I learned about the different areas of death. Learned there's a land in between, so I figure that's where my parents are and that's where my sister was. I knew one day I was destined to find it."

Next thing Agatha knew she was just leaving the bunker right in front of Dorian, and directly behind Dorian was Catherine.

"Like I said, I have something to show you." Zero said extending her arm upward. And the three of them had followed Zero's gesture and they saw all their friends standing high on a podium with leashes around their neck.

Chapter 9

Catherine began screaming and crying her hands went up immediately to her face.

Agatha was in shock, and she just stared off into the distance. Dorian looked around not too sure how to take in the scene, but still he stared on.

"As you can see, this world is mine." Zero said and she began laughing.

Dorian felt the anger inside of him grow, and he remembered his order from the Society. And he looked around he seen some of the members in the crowd of creatures. Then they all started to mutter and mumble a single word, "KILL" but he did not know how, and he was ready for this whole nightmare it and.

As if by magic there came a loud crackling sound, like a firework just went off and it was no more than 5 feet from Dorian's ears! He watched as Zero took a hit and she flew backwards more than 15 feet in the air and fell crashing down hard into the glass shards from the monsters as she had created! Dorian's ears were ringing loudly he could not hear anything, Agatha began tugging on his shirt and he grabbed a hold of Catherine's arm and the three of them ran off with the creatures all confused and trying to figure out what happened.

Dorian Agatha and Catherine passed through creature after creature, and they all moved out of their way. When they finally cleared that the creature path they noticed a young woman standing on the roadway with her arms waving wildly shouting something that they could not hear.

By the time they got to her, their hearing began to clear. She said her name was Rosalynn and she was there to guide them and get them away from the creatures. She handed Dorian a vile and said that this file was the cure.

"All that you have to do is inject this file in to Zero and everything goes back to normal and Zero will float off as a spirit."

"Rosalynn how are we supposed to get back close again without getting turned or caught or trapped?" Asked Dorian.

"You have to use Agatha as bait."

Agatha stepped out of Dorian shadow and looked at Rosalynn and asked Rosalynn how she was supposed to do that when all that she can do is channel spirits. Rosalynn had an answer for this too, "Agatha all that you need to do is channel the spirits of her family that are trapped inside the creatures and when you do, Dorian can stab her with the vile and everything goes back to normal."

Catherine stood behind Dorian and she felt a little uneasy. She tugged gently on Dorian shirt and began muttering something to them, but she couldn't quite make the words come out of her mouth. She put her hand to her head and she felt rather warm this to herself anyway, and suddenly she began to sway back and forth. Agatha got a sneaky suspicion something was wrong, she called it her gut instinct, her woman's intuition and she glanced back at Catherine and noticed that her eyes were no longer her own that they were turning red, crimson.

Rosalynn, Dorian and Agatha all stood back from Catherine. And Dorian watched with amazement as Catherine quickly transformed into the creatures that they've been chased by and watched as she now it, attacked Rosalynn. Rosalynn screamed that Dorian and Agatha to run but she couldn't quite get the word out by the time that the Catherine creature made Rosalynn into one of her.

Dorian took the vile into his pocket and grabbed a hold of Agatha and the two of them ran like their lives depended on it.

Once they got to Monroe Street the two of them stopped and began to look around and noticed that they were no longer being followed. So here they decide to stop and take a breather.

"If you think you can hide from me, you can't." Came Zero's voice like it was over an intercom. Agatha and Dorian looked around for what she was nowhere in sight and the sun was beginning to set they knew that they were in for a long night.

Night 2: that was cold, crisp and as the wind passed by it sent chills up their spines. There was a clothing store on Monroe Street that Dorian knew about and the dumpster behind it that he knew they threw close out for the homeless, so he and Agatha went there. They both found some new jackets that they could wear Dorian found a blue long sleeve jacket look more trench coat, and Agatha's jacket made her look like an Eskimo. They had a good little giggle with her and once the laughing was done they made their way back out on the main street.

Dorian took the vile from the inside of his pants pocket and place it inside the coat pocket and looked at Agatha and said to her that it ends tonight. She nodded her head and they began walking down the street calling Zero's name. They walked three, maybe four blocks without any indication that she was listening or creature interruption, but as soon as they got to the intersection of Munro and Plymouth there they were.

The creatures had surrounded both of them on all sides and they did so in such a hurried fashion that neither Agatha nor Dorian saw them coming. Agatha heard a voice in her head telling her to look up and when she did she saw Zero floating above them. She whispered into Dorian's ear about getting the vile ready and Agatha began to look for Zero's family.

Zero landed right in front of Dorian and reached into his pocket for out the vile and smiled at him.

"This is your big plan. It's not going to work."

"There's only one way to find out Zero," and Dorian yanked the vile out of her hand he popped the top and grabbed a hold of her mouth and plunged the liquid deep into her throat. "This is how will know!"

Zero began coughing and gagging she put her hands up to her throat like she could not breeze, she start smacking at her chest she was pulling on her shirt. Suddenly a light began to shine by her stomach and it was very bright it was a bright white light. And then the light extended down to her feet and then upwards into her arms and into her head. Then they came a massive explosion that shook the entire world and they stood upon and Zero was no more.

The creatures that were infected Dorian watched as they started to become normal again and those that were heavily infected were becoming normal quicker than those that were lightly infected. People were looking at each other left and right trying to figure out where they were and what they were doing there.

Dorian didn't bother for a headcount, he knew that everything was fine again. He looked over at Agatha and he grabbed a hold of her hand and he pulled her in close wrapped his arms around her she in turn wrapped her arms around him, he told her that he loved her, and he gave her a kiss.

Dark clouds began to rise on the horizon and a loud laugh echoed out from them.

"You think you've beaten me? This has only just begun Agatha, Dorian. I will return and you two will be mine!"

Lightning struck the ground in-between Dorian and Agatha and the two of them flew backwards into the arms of hooded strangers who quickly placed cloths overtop of their heads and began dragging them away.

Chapter 10

Agatha had no idea where she was going, nor where she was. All that she knew was that she could not see, and the bag smelt atrocious. She had wondered if Dorian was okay and if the people they saved had seen anything and try to save her. Finally, her car door open and heard two heavy feet touch the pavement.

Agatha heard the shaking of an aerosol can and the marble that bounced all around it and then she felt a mist blow in her face, next thing she knew she was awake in a dark room tied to a chair.

"Agatha," Zero's voice was booming and very boisterous, "did you really think you could defeat me so easily?"

"Why don't you show yourself Zero, untie me and you and I can go rounds and rounds, I'll show you I can defeat you without the need of the vile."

A door open behind Agatha and gave a metal clanging sound as it closed, Agatha heard someone turning on the wheel to lock it and made a very obnoxiously loud squeaking sound. Agatha still could not see anyone in front of her or on her sides, but a sudden pop on the back of her head made her jerk forward and slide her chair forward a couple notches.

Agatha looked at a pair of brown and white tennis shoes and as she started to look up she knows the figure was still in all-black, head to toe even its face was painted black. The only thing she could see the figure in front of her was its emerald green eyes.

"Dorian?"

The figure slapped Agatha across her face. Agatha was ready to cry but she held strong. She did not want to give the figure the satisfaction in knowing that it caused her pain. Agatha was about to open her mouth once more and the figure slapped her again from the other side of her face. Agatha could not fight back the tears and as she sat up the figure watched as they dripped onto her hands.

Agatha heard the door open once more as well as lock once more behind the person who entered in.

"Oh Agatha, you must feel awful about all this." Zero said as she wrapped her hands around Agatha's shoulders. Zero placed her mouth just next to Agatha's ear and whispered something very faintly into it that not even Agatha could hear and the next thing that Agatha knew her body was erect. Zero untied Agatha and told Agatha to stand, sit, punch herself in the gut and the whole time Zero was applauding and laughing. Agatha was in shock inside of herself she had no control over what she was doing to her own body, she was upset that she was some pawn inside of some game Zero was playing.

Agatha was finally given the command to hit the figure in front of her and she hesitated. Zero's looked a little frustrated and commanded once more for Agatha to hit the figure in front of her. Five times Agatha was commanded to do so, and all five times Agatha was unable to comply to Zero's command. Zero had just about enough of her and was about to tell the figure to destroy her when Agatha slapped the figure and sent it back a couple steps.

"Good, about time. I was a little worried about you." Zero said excitedly.

Little did Zero know, but Agatha had begun to break through the spell that she was under and tapped into Zero's thought pattern and was hearing what Zero was planning.

Agatha herself was more than amazed that she could do this, after all, she started out as just a Living Being Channeler and now she's trying to stop Zero from an all-out take over.

Agatha turned to face Zero and the three of them began to walk out the door together.

The walls in the facility that they were in were pale green and beige, the walls looked like they were rusting away at other points. Agatha past by doors and windows that were sealed shut and had black glass on the outside not allowing anyone to view the inside. The floor that they were walking on made a metallic clink to it as they walked even though it was lined with a light red and yellow carpet like material.

They arrived to a door with a bright yellow sun like light illuminating from the bottom of it and as the door opened the figure and Agatha had to take a step back and shield their eyes from the brightness. Agatha turned to get a better look at the figure that had hit her and as the darkness faded from its face she was more shocked and gave away that she was no longer under Zero's control.

"Dorian."

He turned to look at her and he just smiled and with a swift movement of his right hand he sent her flying into the metal wall behind her and Zero turned to look to see what had just happened.

"So, she broke free huh? Good job Dorian." Zero said and began patting Dorian on the head like a dog, "Now, go and begin my revenge and I'll deal with this one personally."

"Like hell you will!" Agatha bolted up from her near crippling position and pushed past Dorian making her way out into the world that she knew.

She stood there in the bright sun light with a huge smile on he face. Her only thought was how the sun felt good versus the darkness that was inside that building. She turned around only to find that the building was no more and the only thing that remained of what she saw was her shadow. Agatha took a few steps toward the area where she once was to make sure it was gone, or it was her imagination playing tricks on her and to her amazement it was gone!

Knowing what was on Zero's mind and her new plan for the world that she loved, Agatha headed toward the road trying to figure out where she was and how to get to someone to help stop this from happening. She wondered the street for a moment or two then figured that she was near Kaki Street and headed west making her way to 401 Dragon Den Blvd.

The buildings and houses were all in rows and nothing seemed out of place and in the daylight, everything looked normal, like nothing from the last two nights had happened. Agatha continued walking on Kaki Street until she hit ran into a roadblock and as she approached the scene she found out that there were no people involved, instead there were animals in the way!

She looked bewildered at this and was not too sure what to make of it. She looked around for the owners and not one person was in the area. So, as she approached (trying to pass) she felt uneasy and the animals seemed to begin to growl at her. Agatha began to think that Zero had done something with all the people they had saved and was now in more of a panic to find someone.

Agatha found herself being able to pass the two dogs that lay in the road and as she passed there was a sense of relief that came over her because they did not attack. She continued walking down Kaki Street for another block or two looking for any sign of life. She found building after building and home after home look like they're void of life and never had any to begin with. Finally, as Agatha passed Grimsley Road, she spied a figure that looked human stumbling up the driveway of one of the homes.

He was tall, slender and as Agatha got closer, she noticed that this figure had blonde hair and blue eyes. He looked feminine to the face, very soft complexion and smooth around the edges. He looked as though he never shaved a day in his life but was obviously not afraid to grow hair if able. He had a copper like skin to his tone and it looked more sprayed on rather than natural and there was a glow about him that looked more heavenly than human.

Agatha crept closer to him, eager to speak to him and yet a little worried that he was something worse and could possibly be an agent from Zero.

"Are you human or other?"

"Human last time I checked. Who are you?"

"Do you know where Dragon Den Blvd is?"

"No. Never heard of it. If you're looking for a bar, I've got just the place for us to go to."

"Not interested."

Agatha turned and walked off and the man stood there puzzled but did not chance after her. Agatha was happy for the fact of finding a human spirit but maddened at the fact that he was of no help.

She made her way back onto Kaki Street and turned right walking toward the west.

The sun was beginning to set, and the wind was just starting to pick up. The trees were rustling in the wind and some were being blown on harder than others. Agatha stopped by a house that had a sign out front that read:

"All Those That Seek Knowledge May Enter Here."

She thought that this maybe a good place to look for a map and possibly rest her head for the night. Agatha walked up to the door and knocked a few times and then jiggled the handle to see if it was locked and found it open. Once inside she began to look around and found the place void of life. There were computers that were on and warm from a day's use, the walls were painted with trees and flowers with little furry animals wondering about, and a set of beds in the far back room. All the rooms looked identical with the paint jobs and it gave a slight joyous feel to her.

Agatha made her way to the first computer and sat in front of it and booted it up.

She was impressed that it was a fast load and running a version of Windows that she was familiar with. She got onto Googles Maps website and searched for 401 Dragon Den Blvd and she found she was seventy miles from it. With no purse or wallet nor money on her she was unsure besides walking how else she was going to get there. That was until a man in a black attire with a white collar stepped into view.

He looked over her shoulder and looked at the map she was looking at and made a mention that he could help her with the help from the local church fund if she had a good story that he could repeat to use on for a Sunday service.

Agatha began to tell the tale of Zero and what she had done to their world and she explained to the collared man that they were dead to begin with and that they were all living a life on this plane like they were living on Earth. The man in the collar just nodded when appropriate and asked only a couple of questions when he deemed that it was necessary. Agatha answered his questions to the best of her ability and found herself feeling more and more comfortable with the man than any other besides Dorian before he killed her. Then she thought about it for a moment, "Why did I kiss him? What was up with that? Was I just relieved?"

The man in the collar walked over to a cabinet and pulled out a set of sheets and a blanket and told her that she could stay the night and that in the morning she could leave with the church's blessings and hope that she finds what she's looking for and defeats Zero.

"If, you need more help, just pray for it and help may arrive in a way that is least expected." He said with a slight rasp to his voice yet still he had a huge smile on his face and he brought comfort to Agatha. Agatha made her bed and asked questions about the building and where she was at, the priest told her that she was in Holly Heights and explained that the building was an old family doctor's office but was redesigned for the church's purpose to help weary travelers whom have gone astray.

"It was a small practice," the priest began, "the good doctor here served about a hundred of us, including me, until he vanished. Some young woman with incredibly long blonde hair driving a red car I think, sat us all down in front of a picture show and it explained that the doctor would not return for some time and that he willed the building to the church."

Agatha had a thought about that blonde girl being Veronica, but she pushed that aside and went about making sure she said good night to the priest and tried her best to get comfy and fall asleep.

During the night Agatha got up and went out looking for a glass of water. She found the priest sitting on a rocking chair in the far back corner of the computer room near the children books and he looked rather pleased with himself. She walked up to him and tapped his shoulder and he jumped a few feet off the chair and looked at her with a surprised look on his face.

"Are you trying to scare me?"

"No, sorry. I was looking for something to drink, do you know where I can find one?"

The man did not get up, he just pointed to a letter and a vile on the counter and said to her that a man in a hooded outfit arrived about an hour ago and delivered it to him and told him to give it to her. The priest debated on whether to do so, but in the end, he just pointed it out and let Agatha make the choice.

She walked over to the vile and the letter and picked them both up and studied them closely. The letter went on to say that she was being watched and that she'd never be able to amass anything toward Zero nor be able to stop her either, so with the vile that was with the letter, it said that she was to take it and forget all her troubles. Agatha threw the vile down and stepped on it until it snapped beneath her feet.

She then bid the priest of farewell and in the cover of night she made her way out the door. The priest soon charged after her and bid her to come back inside and wait until dawn that's when her ride would arrive, but Agatha felt uneasy and was very unsure of the priest. He swore to her that he nor the visitor ever planned on harming her which is why he showed her and gave her the choice and not stopped her. Agatha thought about it for a moment or two and came to realize the same conclusion that the priest meant no harm and followed him back inside.

She did not sleep the rest of the night instead, her in the priest sat and talked. In the morning a yellow taxi cab pulled up in front of the building and honked its horn twice, Agatha showed the priest hand and made her way out to the cab with some money in her pocket from with the priest gave her and told the cab driver where to go.

The drive there was silent, the driver never spoke, and he never turn on the radio.

Agatha looked out on the roadway and knows all the trees of they were passing by in a few buildings and in the next thing she knew they were there.

"Did I fall asleep or something?"

"Yep." And the driver put out his hand looking for change that he had asked her for.

Once she paid them she stepped out of the cab and looked on word to the debilitating building of 401 Dragon Den Blvd. and once more Agatha passed through the archway in the building at once came to life. There was a woman standing in front of the room

10 with red curly hair and she had a broom in her hand with the standard read and black uniform on. Agatha walked up to her and asked if Jack was in and the woman nodded her head and open the door to leader in towards the room where Jack was at.

Jack sat in the ornamental chair and he was reading a book. As Agatha walked, Jack looked up and smiled.

"Welcome back my dear girl." He said as he rose off the chair.

Agatha noticed that he was all in blue and had on a black tie and looked very nice for an old man. He motioned for her to sit next to him on the purple couch and catch up and they talked for some time as Agatha filled him on all the events that she could recall. The next things that Agatha knew, there was a light that began to emit from her hands and it worked down her arms. Jack quickly rose to his feet and took a few steps back and called for someone, meanwhile Agatha's arms spread wide and the light crept up toward her body.

Just as things seemed a little normal, Agatha found herself tied back to the chair in that cold dark room where she was getting slapped in the face by an unknown assailant.

Agatha tried her best to look at the attackers eyes and they were not emerald green like before but brown and looked very sad and depressed, yet at the sometime full of loyalty to whomever this figure worked for.

About The Author

William L. Truax III is a father of two and a disabled Veteran. He served in the United Stated Marine Corps for a short period of time and was injured and sent home. He lives in Marianna, FL and enjoys his time with his family. He wishes for everyone to have a great day and enjoy their time with their loved ones.

www.ingramcontent.com/pod-product-compliance
Ingram Content Group UK Ltd.
Pitfield, Milton Keynes, MK11 3LW, UK
UKHW022223230426
12048UKWH00016BA/1026